Stephen Fawcett

Bradford Legends

Stephen Fawcett

Bradford Legends

ISBN/EAN: 9783337152758

Printed in Europe, USA, Canada, Australia, Japan

Cover: Foto ©Andreas Hilbeck / pixelio.de

More available books at **www.hansebooks.com**

A COLLECTION OF

BY STEPHEN FAWCETT,

Author of "Wharfedale Lays," "Edwy and Elgiva," &c., &c:

Methinks it were not much to die,
To die and leave behind
A spirit in the hearts of men,
A voice amid our kind.

L. E. L.

BRADFORD:

C. DENTON, MACHINE PRINTER, SUN-BRIDGE.

1872.

To

MATTHEW WILLIAM THOMPSON, ESQ.,

UPON WHOM, BRADFORD, (HIS NATIVE BOROUGH), HAS CONFERRED
THE HIGHEST HONORS IN ITS POWER, THIS WORK IS HUMBLY
INSCRIBED BY

THE AUTHOR.

PREFACE.

A few observations on *divine romance* will be perhaps the best preface to a work like this. Anything that has no touch of the finger of romance in it, is saltless and insipid to the mental palate. In romance we project great achievements,— noble deeds are done,—speculations are founded and reared into what are called aerial castles,—we dwell in palaces and crack wi' kings. Few are aware that those aerials are often realized in the external, and that that which is but an unsubstantial vision of the present, may be a substantial reality of the future.

Romance is the Eden of the mind—those who have never revelled in it are expelled from Paradise, for it is the beauty of spirit-land—the happiness to come. In the eyes of the wholly practical and unromantic man who seeks only for gain, like the beast that seeks only for food, Salem, Thebez, Athens, and Tadmor, are only bare unsightly mounds, broken columns, and mouldering desolate tombs of the past, to be avoided. But to the romantic the clangour of war—the pipe of peace—the voices of the conqueror, the law giver, the sophist, and the poet, are yet heard—the dead and half-buried ruins of magnificence erect themselves again in all the glory of their prime.

Music and song are but the utterances of the romance of love. Cheerless and cold are the souls which have no flowers, no ornaments, no gilding within them. The mighty power of oratory and all the amenities of civilization are from romance. Scotland, for instance, in itself barren and cold, has become a land of the highest interest, beautified and warmed by its histories, memorials, and melodies. We care not to visit parvenu and upstart towns and cities which have not been hallowed and mantled by the romance of the past—where men long gone have not left their shadows on every wall and monument—where the mighty dead return not.

America and Australia have little romance as yet, but their poets, musicians, and novelists are busy weaving its magic web. We reck not to visit the Me-chacebe as we do the Jordan—the streams of the Eurotas and the Tweed have greater interest than the Yarrayarra or the Orinoco.

Our soberest lives themselves assume a weirdly form in the haze of the past, and reality begins to dissolve into the mellowed sadness of unreality.

The fabled gardens of Alcinous and of Armida are but images of the aspirations of the soul,—creations of unfulfilled desires, like the heaven of the christians, and the happy hunting grounds of the denizen of the desert.

History, Biography, Astronomy, and the Narratives of Travellers and Naturalists are dry, insipid, and tiresome, without the charm that is found in the inspired language of the poet and novelist, who see romance revealed only to their ken.

Unfathomable man, the romantic work of the Deity, goeth forth in happy summer and in cheerless winter to reveal to himself by correspondence, the mysteries of the romance of his being and his love, and returns to his rest in the hope of its enchantment, in the visions and dreams of the night.

S. F.

POEMS.

THE QUEEN IN SWITZERLAND.

——:o:——

THE widowed Queen of mount and main
   Sailed o'er the German sea,
In royal yacht with all her train
   For Switzerland the free.

Haste, Stanley, haste from revelry
   Imperial Fontainebleau,
And from Eugenie's witchery,
   Thou loyal lord and true.

Thy sovereign chides thy fond delay,
   Nor does she chide in vain ;
For soon within her chatelet
   Thou'rt by her side again.

STANLEY.

What, still in silent grief, my Queen,
   In the glorious land of Tell,
Where peace now waves her olive green
   O'er fields where tyrants fell?

Lo, yonder Magnates high from Berne,
   And Inspruck's pipers come,
And the bold battalions of Lucerne
   Awake the northern drum ;

And see my Queen Helvetia teems
   Her offerings at thy shrine,
Thee in ambition's summer dreams
   Beheld as half divine.

Wherever rolls yon orb of day,
   Wherever ocean rolls
Thy banners wave—thy gentle sway
   But bounded by the poles.

Then why in silent grief, my Queen,
  In the glorious land of Tell,
Where freedom's brand is still as keen
  As when Burgundia fell?

THE QUEEN.

Hold, Stanley, hold! In " Vesper hymn,"
  And " Ranz des vaches " song,
I only hear the voice of him,
  Of him I've mourned so long.

STANLEY.

O'er Righi's snows the eagle sails,
  Olympian splendours see ;
There are a thousand nightingales
  In Val di Chamounix ;

The orange bloom is in the light,
  The Alps with rose tints shine ;
And yonder dancing are the bright
  Young Nereiads of the Rhine ;

Sweet Belgium's Queen to thee shall sing,
  Shall strew thy couch with flowers,
And England's matrons' blessings wing,
  To speed the golden hours.

Take cheer of heart my liege ladye,
  Restrain thy sorrows' flow ;
Thine is not Helle's Niobe,
  Nor childless Rachel's woe.

Thy children fondly round thee cling,
  A fair and princely throng,
To happier climes thy Consort-king
  Shall welcome thee ere long.

THE QUEEN.

Stanley, my throne's vast height I know,
  And all conspire to cheer;
And the rays of heaven would gild my brow
  If Albert were but here.

Away ! My British bugles blow,
  Away my royal train ;
My sovereign duty calls, and ho !
  For Albion's hills again.

A DREAM OF PEEL PARK.

——:o:——

I DREAMT, and, behold, in the car of Queen Mab,
  I was borne to a beautiful glade,
Weird and elfin and sheen, pearly golden and green,
  Where I walked with my favourite maid.

The wind piped a tune from the note-book of June,
  And the fountains and rivulets sighed;
And the young linnet flew round the linden and yew,
  Singing sweetly, in search of his bride.

The classic acanthus and old polyanthus
  On tiptoe, with sunflowers, sprang;
To the throstle, the lark, over lovely Peel Park,
  High, exulting in heaven's vault, sang.

" My beloved is true, but is far, far away,
  Over yonder blue hills of the morn,"
Sighed an exotic bright, as a butterfly white
  Fanned and pitied the exile lovelorn.

From each flower sprang a nymph of the clime of her birth,—
  There were nymphs from Columbia there,
From the Nile's burning land, and from far Samarcand,
  And from dreamy Cathay and Cashmeer.

There came fairies from Bowling, and houris from Horton,
  And witches from Manningham lea;
There were Psyche and Zoe, and Daphne and Chloe,
  And an elfin queen's lovers levee.

And the sun hung his robe of red gold on the banks,
  Till th' imperial moon came up fair,
In her bright maiden zone; but she came not alone
  In her search for Endymion there.

And the lilac and golden laburnum shook hands
  With the sorrow-born cypress tree;
And the breeze kissed the bowers, and the bees kissed the flowers
  And Sweetwilliam kissed Rosamarie.

But the winds, warblers, fountains, and leaflets were hushed,
  As the elfin queen sang from the grove:
" Weary Bradford, rest here from terrestrial care,
  And here keep thy ledger of love."

I awoke, but the glamour still shadowed my soul,
  And 'twas long ere the vision decayed;
For I still heard the lark over bonny Peel Park,
  Still I walked with my favourite maid.

A ROYAL HYMENEAN.

——:o:——

Heard ye the news that came the morn,
Royalty weds the Lord o' Lorn ;
Inverary will busk her braw,
Mutchkins o' mountain dew will fa',
Mull will roar wi' a milder strain,
Skye and Iona grow green again ;
Wingless bonnets will fly in the clan,
Nane sae blythe as the Highlandman.

What has he whisper'd in beauty's lug ?
Had he the Cupid's cantrip drug ?
Spoke he o' deeds o' the olden time,
Sung he in Gaelic or Lowland rhyme ?
Kent he the weird o' spaewife's gab,
Reach for an apple an' no for a crab ?
Hearts never faint in the Campbell clan,
Bold is the raid of the Highlandman.

Southern lords hae rich domains,
Southern carls hae fertile plains,
Southern dukes are proud and great,
High on the cliff is the Campbell's seat.
He wons with the eagle in glen and ravine,
Then hoo did he woo an' hoo did he win ?
Proud are the hearts of the Campbell clan,
Germans will squint at the Highlandman.

The bonniest bud of the rose has sworn
Her troth to the Lord o' the Isles o' Lorn ;
She comes to the land o' the tartan kilt,
To the castle by Morvens heroes built ;
She comes to the lilt, to the pibroch's din,
But hoo did the laddie the princess win ?
Ask an' ye will guess an' ye can,
Ye kenna the spunk o' a Highlandman.

Goody ye've bakit the bannocks the noo,
Doon wi' your knitting and taits o' woo.
Don your new plaidie and kurtchy braw,
Jenny is rinning wi' Rab to the ha' ;
Ae glint at the wench will be good for the een,
Her bairnies will hae for their grannie a Queen.
The pluck o' a Scot is nae flash in the pan,
There's luck in the lot o' the Highlandman.

THE BARON OF BIERLEY HALL.

——:o:——

When the forest full dressed in its cymar of green,
  Heard the ringdove and partridge's call,
Will Scarlett, disguised as a crusader old,
  Grey-bearded, and burly and tall,
Blew a blast on the horn at the barbican gate
  Of the Baron of Bierley Hall.

" Now what is thy will," growled the seneschal rough,
  Coming here at the dusk of the eve ?"
A cup of small ale and a bed for the night,
  By the Baron of Bierley's leave ;
For the sake of the blest holy rood thou wilt not
  A poor pilgrim from Palestine grieve."

" Come in now, come in," said the Baron, " my frere ;
  And thy tale I will presently hear.
But what hast thou got in the bag at thy back ?"
  " 'Tis a rebeck, my lord, that I bear."
" Then give me a fytte," quoth the Baron, well pleas'd,
  And I warrant thee lodging and cheer !"

The Baron's fair daughter smiled pleasantly on,
  And listened Will's troubadour song ;
'Twas the strain she had rambled the greenwood to hear,
  From a known and right musical tongue ;
And her neck match'd the ruby that burn'd in her hair,
  And her gaze was keen-searching and long.

" Now tell me thy tale of King Richard's bold deeds,
  And Ascalon's Paynims afar :
My daughter I've pledged to a crusader knight,
  Noble, old, and disabled by war."
And the Baron drank sack as a nobleman should
  Until midnight look'd down with her star.

At length in his revel the Baron began
  To nod till, like tempest, he snor'd ;
Then a tale of true love in the maid's willing ear
  Will Scarlet right gallantly poured ;
And soon on a pillion behind him she sat,
  And to merry green Sherwood they scour'd.

The Baron awoke at the crack of the day,
  No Cicely answered his call ;
And soon he found out that the maid was away
  With the soldier grey-bearded and tall ;
And fearful and fierce was the anger's display
  Of the Baron of Bierley Hall.

THE BARON OF BIERLEY HALL.

PART SECOND.

Bierley's baron sat sad and forlorn,
  His daughter abducted and gone,
When a conjurer blew a loud mot at his gate,
  And begged in mysterious tone
To spell him his rede and forwarn him his weird
  Ere his star's benign aspect was gone.

"Come in, friend, come in," roared the baron in wrath,
  "At least I've no daughter to lose,
Read me soothly her fate, or with tough ashen staff
  All the bones in thy carcase I'll bruse."
"Thy threats I disdain," quoth the conjurer bold,
  For I deal not in charlatan ruse."

Then slowly he lifted his magical wand,
  And pointed east, west, north, and south,
And the baron looked grave upon seeing his book
  And his figures unknown and uncouth.
Three notes on his bugle the conjurer blew,
  Sharp and shrill, as if blown by a youth.

Instantly coming from copse, wood, and bush,
  Full a hundred tall archers were seen,
And a knight in bright harness rode boldly in front,
  With a lady and page at his rein,
And soon they all stood at the barbican gate,
  Knight and lady, and bowmen in green.

"Go forth, thou bold baron, go presently forth,
  For yonder stands Lincoln's proud son,
De Lacy, of Bradford and Horton the heir,
  And of Alnwick, both tower and town;
Thy Cicely now is his beautiful bride.
  So lately abducted and gone."

Then up went the baron's big hand, and he smote
  On his buck-leather breeches a smack,
Knocked his seneschal down for a sturdy old churl,
  With a heavy and terrible thwack,
And his benizon gave to the conjurer, by
  A huge sledge-hammer slap on his back.

"Come in, now, come in," called the baron aloud,
  "Heave up the portcullis and gate,
My daughter is welcome, with husband and train,
  For I trow she has changed her mate,

And her knight cannot be the grey-bearded old knave,
  With his cozening music and prate."

Then in marched Will Stukeley and Adam and Mutch,
  Friar Tuck and young Allan á dale,
And Little John burly with cudgel in hand,
  That had oft made his enemies quail;
And the baron, amazed, marked the bowmen all bend
  To the conjurer ancient and pale.

"Now, what is thy name," asked the baron, in doubt,
  "That the yeomen all bend and obey,
Tell me sooth, and a hundred gold nobles are thine,
  For thy wonderful magic to-day."
"I am y'cleped Robin Hood, I am Huntingdon's earl,
  And in merry green Sherwood I stay."

"Set abroach every barrel of berry brown ale,
  Fill the quaighs for the foresters all,
Stay and dine, my bold fellow, and shake the old roof
  With thy bully boys proper and tall."
And the nobles drank sack as all noblemen should,
  With the Baron of Bierley Hall.

A LEGEND OF POPE GREGORY VIII.

——:o:——

THE raving wind and hurtling shower,
In the hurricane's most dismal hour
  Of mountain-wrath, roared hideously;
When in his cell, on Bernard's side,
To pleasure and the world denied,
O'er the lone life long winters tried,
  Mused the young hermit Gregory.

Suddenly his thoughts found words:
" Are some of fair creation's lords
  Thus doom'd by heaven to waste in vain
Life's vernal days in praise and prayer,
Lone penitents, starved, cold and bare,
Whilst others sumptuously fare
  Unused to penury or pain?

" 'Tis false ! No more this life I'll lead—
Ye Saints no more your wrath I dread—
  I'll seek the busy world once more !

Away, ye lying volumes all !
Give me the gorgeous palace hall,
Where varied joys and pleasures call,
　　From banquet room to lady's bower !"

His lamp flared blue—his fire burned low,
Care brooded on his gloomy brow,
　　Weird fancies mocked his troubled mind ;
When screams rose on the furious breeze,
And laughs that caused his blood to freeze,
And oaths and broken sentences
　　Mixed wildly with the angry wind.

Yet Gregory feared not, for his soul
Was brave—his head in danger cool.
　　The blast dashed ope his little door ;
In walked a form with haughty stride,
Mirk as the night : with mien of pride,
And wondering Gregory fiercely eyed,
　　And stood before him on the floor.

Now Gregory seize thy beads and book,
There's something in that stranger's look
　　May mortal courage put to proof !
He spoke—" I come a friendly guest,
Why here dost idly musing rest,
And lose young years the brightest, best,
　　Unloved beneath this wretched roof ?

" Accept this cloak—its every fold
Was woven by bald priests of old,
　　In cloistered gloom and mystery ;
Throw its dark folds about thy limbs—
Ne'er do it off—in it sing hymns,
Wake, sleep, or perpetrate thy crimes—
　　The garment's named Hypocrisy.

" Look yonder !"—Gregory turned his eye,
And, towering to Italia's sky,
　　The Vatican and seven-hill'd Rome
Arose in blue infernal light.—
" Down, Gregory, kneel, adore my might ;
And more than rises to thy sight
Is thine—for I can give the right—
　　The Pontiff's crown shall thine become !"

That cloak Avernian, Gregory took,
And knelt.—The hill beneath him shook ;
　　The arch-fiend laughed and disappear'd.
The hermit left his lonely cell,

Of grace bereft and school'd by hell,
And went in cities fair to dwell
  And saint and sage to kings appeared.

Anon, where Tiber laves his strand
In old Ausonia's tawny land,
  Pope Gregory's three tiaras blaze,
And monarchs tremble at his scowl,
And nations pale as thundering roll
  His bullas and anathemas.

THE WILD BOAR OF BRADFORD.

——:o:——

The wild boar of Bradford was huge and immense,
No woodman could turn him with cudgel or fence;
He rooted up trees, trampled down corn and cole,
Ripp'd oxen and horses and swallow'd them whole;
He ate up an apple wife, tough, old and tall,
And crunch'd up her wheelbarrow, trundle and all.

Boar-hounds were useless, he snapp'd them up quick;
For gripes, spears and arrows his hide was too thick.
On a Capuchin friar he one morn broke his fast,
And the monks of St. Peter's stood staring aghast,
And concluded to send for St. Dunstan divine,
For the demon again had got into a swine.

Down came the blacksmith with hammer and tongs,
To settle with Satan for manifold wrongs;
Holy water in blessed sanctgraal he got,
And his crosier took in his perilous plot;
For Spinkwell he hurried, and when he came there,
Found the brawn, unsuspecting, asleep in his lair.

The first thing he did was to spill from sanctgraal,
Holy wet on his tusks, and his ears, and his tail,
Thrust his crosier, as 'twere but a common cole runt,
In his stern end, and up woke the boar with a grunt
And a yell, startling deer upon Wibsey's wild slack,
And fled with St. Dunstan, like knight on his back.

He kick'd, snorted, gambol'd, leap'd, gallop'd, and ran,
But with hammer and tongs Dunstan sat like a man;
To dislodge his bold rider, through thorn, brake, and bush,
Through dingle and dell he made dart, start and rush,

Through Shipley's dense wood, and up Eldwick's glen made,
Snorting, screaming, and grunting, nor slackened nor stayed.

A hunter by Sampson's old thorn saw them pass,
Tongs in hand, holy Dunstan was singing a mass,
And the ghost of Tom Rumbalds sat on his stone chair,
At the bristling steed and his rider to glare ;
No saddle had Dunstan, no bridle's weak thongs,
But with hammer and tongs he rode—hammer and tongs.

On his nightmare a grim rider joined them in black,
And a sowgelder's horn winded loud in the track ;
Helter skelter the barghcist and bandogs are out,
Old Lancha's bogs quak'd with demoniac shout ;
Dunstan's brawn kept the lead, grunting, foaming, and quick,
All sunk in the hollow of Whinney-i'th-nick !

From that day to this, in the hill-tempest's clamour,
May be heard the loud ring of a stithy and hammer;
And 'tis given out by shepherds, among other tales,
That St. Dunstan is sharpening Sathanas his nails,
And his horns and his pitchfork, to win with more ease,
A duello wager with John of Kirklees.

THE BLACK DUEL OF KIRKLEES.

"Barney bang'd Banagher and Banagher bang'd the D——l."

GHOSTLY. unctuous, and holy, sat John at his ease,
Awaiting his foe in the church of Kirklees ;
Sacred wine down his gullet with gusto he dribbled,
And oft at some bread consecrated he nibbled,
When a clanking he heard in the Abbey's dark nave,
And smelt brimstone-fumes mix'd with stench of the grave,
And hastily rising th' intruder to see—
Met Satan who made him a haughty *congee.*

"Sit down," said stout John, "state the mode of our duel,
For war has its laws, be it ever so cruel ;
Let Priap and imp stand aside for the nonce,
Choose thy weapons and let us go at it at once !"
Quoth Satan, "the weapons are three I delight in,
Their invention I claim—tippling, gambling, and fighting."

"I accept all the three, and first, Gambling, said John ;
"Here are dice—shake them up—I have loaded not one.
Fifty souls, if I win, purgatorial pains
Shall escape, and mine own is thy prize if thou gains."
"It is settled," quoth Satan, loud rattling the cup,
"And remember, my friend, it is forty of up."

As they play'd, round them corpse-lights burned red, white,
   and blue,
And the abbey's ghosts gather'd the black game to view;
With confidence John rattled, tumbled and toss'd,
And Satan play'd, grinning and swearing,—and lost;
And, stamping his club-foot, his pitchfork he shook,
And John his oak sapling courageously took.—

"Have at thee!" cried he, and let fly at his head,
And Satan fell down with the blow as if dead;
One horn and his pitchfork were broken in twain,
He'd been brain'd (had he brains), and he bellow'd with pain:
"I'll give in!" he roar'd out, "thou hast well won this bout,
Thy quaterstaff drop, and the bottle bring out."

Their measures were equal, the vintage the same,
They gulped equal draughts, and sung songs at the game;
And they boozed seven hours, until Satan, unable
To drink any more, tumbled under the table—
But woke in a trice, and exclaimed, "I am done—
Take the souls, and bo d—d to thy pluck, Prior John!"

Quoth John, "from henceforth never monk will be found,
But at all these three games will hold stoutly his ground.
Shake hands, my old beauty!" and seizing his foe,
Crush'd his claws till he winc'd, and then, laughing, let go;
"I will tell thee," said he, the "true cause of thy foil,
I greased my hands well with some thrice holy oil."
Papa Satan look'd jack-knives, his blue cheeks inflated,
Strode his wing'd old red dragon and absquatulated.

JOAN OF ARC.

Joan of Arc, called also La Pucelle and the Maid of Orleans, was a peasant girl of Domremi, in Lorraine, who in the disastrous state of affairs in France that followed the death of Henry V., fired by patriotic and religious enthusiasm, undertook to deliver the city of Orleans, on which the last hope of Charles VII. hung, then besieged by the English. She succeeded, and compelled the besieged to retire, and afterwards had Charles solemnly crowned at Rheims.

The arrow whistled o'er the trench, the ramparts blazing blue,
Death's volleying iron thunder belched, and murder's missiles
   flew;
Old Orleans trembled to her base, as charging English steel
Flash'd ruddily mid cannons roar and huge balista's peal—
When mid the din proud Talbot cried, "Give back! for
   driving on,
A hostile army comes!" nor dreamt of fierce Domremi Joan.

Resistless, as down Alpine heights the avalanches crash,
On reeking chargers galloping through serried spears they dash,
"Say, whose is yon grand form in mail," asked Talbot, turning
    pale ;"
"He rides as if his horse was borne on fierce tornado gale ;"
His captains deem'd, but durst not say, Saint Denis had come
    down
To head the chivalry of France, but 'twas Domremi Joan.

A moment, and bold Talbot's sword was broken to the hilt,
A moment, and a cataract of English blood was spilt ;
A moment, and their shatter'd files for safety rode and ran
Before that bright bold leader's lance, careering in the van.
"A woman !" cried the officers, and Talbot heaved a groan,
"Death ! shall I for a woman fly ?" but 'twas Domremi Joan.

From Orleans' granite battlements the people saw afar
The English host beleaguering bend before the storm of war ;
The mother holding up her child, cried, "See, my lov'd one,
    see !
Our foes disperse like Arden's deer, and La belle France is free !"
Proud Talbot cross'd the sea enraged, and nearly all alone,
Like lion foil'd by maiden's hand,—Domremi's mighty Joan.

Forth from the city noble lord and knight, and high-born dame,
To meet that wondrous woman in grand procession came.
With oriflamme unfurl'd, behold the Royal Charles advance,
As drum and trumpet heralded the prodigy of France ;
He led the maid through regal halls, he led her to his throne,
And princes bent their haughty crests before Domremi Joan.

JOAN OF ARC.

Joan of Arc, otherwise La Pucelle, was taken by the party of the
Duke of Burgundy and sold to the English, who, after the formality of
a trial, burnt her alive as a witch in 1431, aged about 20 years.

The death-stake was ready, the faggots were piled,
The chaunt of the monks rising woful and wild,
Red flambeaux around shed a baleful dead light ;
And star-spangles studded the dome of the night
When Warwick on horseback in hauberk and plume
Commanded fair Joan to be led to her doom.

Her robe painted over with demons and flames,
Was labelled with " witch," " hag," and other foul names,
Bent down like the lily, bedew'd with its tears,

She hid her wan face with her shame and her fears;
Bound fast with rude hands in old damp rusted chains,
The blood started blue to her delicate veins.

On a throne, flashing gold, sat the Legate of Rome,
With pennon and cross looming dim in the gloom,
While cries of " Die sorceress " rose from the throng
Of thousands above the bald Carmelites' song;
And the faggots were fired, when a thunderclap broke
Overhead with the first curling column of smoke.

The " cynosure "* blazed and enlarg'd in the north,
And with lightning a chariot of silver sent forth,
Rushing down through the blue like a meteor it came,
And the fires of its axles streak'd heaven with flame;
Its rider the Virgin—One flash of her eye
Quench'd the pile and struck prostrate the guards standing by.

" Hail victrix," she said, and she caught the Pucelle,
In her arms—and her anklets and manacles fell,
And the maiden unharm'd up to heaven she bore,
And the " cynosure " opened and closed as before.
A miracle! shouted the Legate and train,
A miracle! thunder'd the people again,
When a blind Bradford heretic's voice from the crowd,
('Twas Hugo de Lacy's) roar'd " Well I'll be blow'd."

A LEGEND OF KNARESBRO' FOREST.

——:o:——

" Where art thou going, sweet shepherdess,
    Where art thou going so early?"
" My flocks I feed in Havarah's mead,
    When dew is shining clearly."

" Drop of dew or starry blue
    Never knew such beauty;
Havarah's maid I came to wed,
    But love has conquer'd duty."

" Ride on, ride on, De Lacy bold,
    I trust no traitorous lover;
My low degree were shame to thee,
    I fear thou art a rover!"

" Lord Dacre's child I will not wed,
    By heaven I've sworn already;

* The north star.

B

Of castle, town, and dale and down,
  Thou only shalt be lady."

" Ride on, ride on !" she archly cried,
  " For I soothly vow and fairly,
No shepherdess shalt thou caress,
  Should'st love, and e'er so dearly :

Lord Dacre is a gruesome carle,
  To ruth and fear a stranger ;
But wizards say love hears no Nay—
  Be thine the shame and danger !"

He merrily placed her on his steed,
  Tripp'd like a page beside her,
And with glancing stream, and dewdrop beam,
  Merrily glanced the rider.

He placed her on his palfrey proud,
  And sought a hermit's dwelling,
Where, kneeling, he in sanctity
  His rosary was telling.

The hermit rose and wedded them,
  O'er holy missal bending ;
Sweet strains of love from Havarah's grove
  On morning's wings ascending.

Thou art beguiled," cried the shepherdess,
  As in his arms he caught her,
" Thy oath and word are broke, false lord,
  I am Lord Dacre's daughter !"

De Lacy gazed, confused, amazed,
  Upon the lovely speaker ;
And the captive now was led to bow
  Before the great Lord Dacre.

AUMOUSCLIFFE : A ROMAUNT.

Aumouscliffe, or Almscliff, is one of the most beautiful objects in Wharfedale, being crowned as it were with a rocky diadem and containing a subterranean passage leading, as some of the neighbouring villagers believe, into the regions of fairyland. It is well deserving a visit from the lovers of natural romance.

'Twas the hour when in Riffa the fallow-deer hide,
  And Washburn forms cascade and linn,
That De Lacy alone with his bright virgin bride
A portal espied upon Aumouscliff's side,
  And a varlet, who bid them walk in.

" Whose servitor, thou ?" quoth De Lacy, " I pray,
   For I ken but a gateway and thee."
" 'Tis the fairy king's palace : his daughter to day
In marriage he gives to an Indian fay,
   And invites you the spousals to see."

" Lead on," said De Lacy, " I long for the sight,"
   And the door opened wide with a bang,
And a vast pillar'd hall full of spangles of light,
Blazed round them with garlands and jewels bedight.
   And eldritch wild laughter peals rang.

To dances of fauns, afrits, elfins burlesque,
   Played fifty horned pipers in green ;
De Lacy they honoured with greetings grotesque,
And high on a dais of gold arabesque
   King Oberon sate with his queen.

In the presence, with crown of flame spiral, bright red,
   Stood the Monarch of India's son ;
And the king's blushing daughter before him was led,
In mirth, song, and music the marriage rite sped,
Then off like a flash, on their wedding tour fled
   The pair to see old " Prester John."

Then the king raised his wand, and the silence, to hear
   His majesty's hest, was profound ;
And he spoke, as he lifted his goblet in air,
" From my cup never drained drink a health to the fair—
   Drink *wisdom*, and let it go round."

Round and round bir'd the bowl, till its circuit was made,
   And De Lacy drank deep with his bride ;
And the palace was gone, and they found themselves laid
In each other's embrace, in a witch-hazel's shade,
   Upon haunted old Anmouscliff's side.

A bugle's wild blast in green Riffa they heard,
   And arose at the soul-stirring sound ;
And a full score of nobles and damsels appeared,
And lusty Lord Dacre the barony cheered
   With halloos unto falcon and hound.

DE LACY,

To Charles Turner, Esq., Idle.

Childe Roland to the dark tower came,
His word was still " Fee, fo, fum,
I smell the blood of a British man."—King Lear.

Fnt brt nvr wn fr bly.—Ld Sw.

In feudal days, when William's men
   Came clinking o'er from Normandy,

A castle stood in upland glen,
    Where goblins held high revelry.

The sun rose there with drowsy eyes,
    In morning robes of misty grey,
And took night's lanthorn from the skies,
    And yawning ask'd the time o' day ?

Sleep and sloth chain'd young and old,
    Clowns with owls would wink and sit ;
The lazy Aire beneath it roll'd,
    And Bradford calls it Idle* yet.

De Lacy to that dark tower came,
    Where dwelt the Lady Erminie :
Ten Saxon knights of stalwart frame,
    Had fallen by her sorcery.

Three hung themselves on cornel tree,
    Three widows box'd three others' ears,
Transmogrified to beer casks three,
    And one dissolved away in tears.

De Lacy, curtal axe in hand,
    Bang'd boldly on the castle gate,
And in he stalk'd with dag and brand,—
    A bell toll'd—dead lights' hurried fate.

Ten mailed forms stood round the hall,
    Like trophies in an armoury ;
Each clashed his arms as rung his call
    " Lead me to Lady Erminie."

In tone sepulchral outspoke one ;
    " Our lady sleeps within her bower ;
One errant knight, her demons own,
    Can disenchant her pagan tower.

That knight alone may kiss her lip,
    And break her magic wand and spell ;
But if he fears its dew to sip—
    He dies." Bang ! clang'd again the bell.

Bars clash'd, and iron doors flew back,—
    A shining dragon near him stood ;
Turrets tremble, pillars crack,
    Danger cools not gentle blood.

There was a smack—no dragon hiss'd,
    But changed its form, and strange to see,
The monster's lip the knight had kiss'd,
    Was own'd by Lady Erminie.

    * A small town near Bradford, Yorks.

All honour to the Norman knight,
  Who won the lady and her dower;
All honour to the brave in fight,
  And gallant in a lady's bower.

DE LACY.

Under the De Lacies there undoubtedly existed here (*i.e.*, in Hall Ings, Bradford) a castle or castlet.—*James's History of Bradford.*

DE LACY rode forth to the wars of the north,
  To set the blue bonnets in order;
And a troth he received and a lady believed
  Ere he followed the drum o'er the border.

Scotch limbs he contused, and got battered and brused
  By moss-troopers, raiders, and rievers;
In skirmish he fought, and withstood the onslaught
  Of fierce clans, with their claymores and cleavers.

But his crown got a clour, when the blood of the flower
  Of broad Scotland to puddle was trodden,
When James with the pride of his chivalry died
  In the terrible battle of Flodden.

Then of sowens and jannocks, cold crowdy and bannocks
  And kebbucks and drummocks aweary,
He with noble and train came to England again,
  Over peat-hag and wilderness dreary.

It was eve when he came to the tower of the dame
  Whose glove in his helmet he'd carried.
She, seeing him nigh, cried from balcony high,
  " De Lacy, avaunt thee! I'm married!"

Faint and wounded he turned, and his lot inly mourned,
  And to none spoke a cheerful or sad word;
Fearful silence he kept, drank a cruisckin and slept
  In his cold gloomy castle at Bradford.

Did he seek the moat deep, take the lover's last leap,
  Court death in the wars o'er the billow?
Or in hermitage quiet make cresses his diet,
  His head crowned with withy and willow?

Did he murmur his care to the wild desert air,
  Or sit in the sulks with his mother?
No! Dan Cupid to spite, he (a sensible knight)
  Went to Court to look out for another!

PITY POOR BRADFORD.

This ghost story has been given in the "Genuine Account," namely, that the Earl of Newcastle being in bed at Bowling Hall, an apparition appeared to him and importuned him with these words:—"Pity poor Bradford"—"Pity poor Bradford." Newcastle having charged his men to kill all—man, woman, and child—in the town, and give them Bradford quarter, for the brave Earl of Newport's sake.—*James's History of Bradford.*

HER bright silver arrow Diana shot down,
Over leaguering army, and terror-struck town,
  Through the casement of Adela's bower ;
Where lovely but wan as the snow on the hill,
Or the lily storm-smit on the verge of the rill,
  She won'd in the wind-beaten tower.

" Haste thee, Mysie, my tire-maid ! 'tis late, girl, 'tis late
My bridegroom is ready—he knocks at the gate—
  The hour of my bridal is near—
My bracelets, my cincture, my coronet gay,
Gold, ruby, and diamond, shall deck my array,
  For the sake of young Newport, my dear."

Her bower-woman shuddered in fear and dismay ?
" Dear lady," she murmur'd, " bethink thee, I pray,
  In the chapel he lies cold and dead."
" It is false, simple maid, he surviv'd the dread fight,
The banquet is waiting, the cressets shine bright,
The minstrels are ready with music's delight,
  Seek thy pallet and be not afraid."

  .   .   .   .

In the stillness of night Newcastle saw with affright
His curtains withdrawn in the ghastly moonlight,
  And a phantom as ghastly and pale,
With a zone round its breast and with arm and head tires
Flashing, burning and ruddy, with circling fires,
And a wimple of mist for a veil.

With his heart in his throat the Earl gasp'd " What art thou,
Disturber of rest ?" As the windharp's tone low,
  As a seraph's sweet accents he heard,
" Pity poor Bradford !" in suppliant strain—
" Pity poor Bradford !" more piteous again—
  And the vision in gloom disappear'd.

Ere the daystar arose upon camp and vidette,
Rose the Earl with command for an instant retreat,
  And the tongue that but yesterday swore
Bradford quarter to all the doom'd town should be given

Was false and foresworn unto vengeance and heaven
    And Newport was left in his gore !

But Bowling's dim halls heard a cry and a wail,
In the chapel two corpses lay silent and pale ;
    Lady Adela, trimm'd like a bride,
In the stiffen'd embrace of young Newport the brave,
Lay awaiting her nuptial couch in the grave
    With her hero to sleep by her side.

ST. CRISPIN AND OLD NICK.

——:o:——

Hob Crispin sat whacking a sole on his stall,
Then threw down his sole, hammer, lapstone and awl ;
The hot sultry weather caused sweat drops to roll—
" That the Dule," he exclaimed, " had both lapstone and sole !"
Old Nick, hearing this, in his studio below,
Rose, presto, to see what the dule was to do.

He stood before Crispin, with tail over arm ;
"Good morn !" greeted he, "You appear rather warm,
I heard with your soul you just now wished to part,
And the price, if I buy, is —each wish of your heart ;
Five years to enjoy and to live shall be thine,
Then the bargain shall be that thy soul shall be mine."

" Done !" quoth the cobbler, and snatched up his pen,
Drew blood for his ink, and his terms drew up then—
" *At the end of five years having all I can wish
Old Nick has my sole !* Now will that do, old fish ?
"That will do," replied Nick, " Now have all thy desire,
The bond I will hold ;" and he vanished in fire.

The first thing Hob Crispin much wished for he got,
A peck of pease-porridge came hot in a pot ;
Then he wished that his pockets were all full of gold ;
And they filled in a moment full as they could hold,
Then he wished for a noble's embroidered suit,
And one ready-made bundled right to his foot.

Said he, " Now, I'll see Rome and forthwith see the Pope.
    And fill him his hampers, his pokes, and his bags,
When he's glutted a right merry evening, I hope,
    I shall spend with his primates and cardinal wags ;
So to Rome he sped fast as an arrow can fly,
And the Pope he found musing and cocking his eye.

He filled all the chests that his holiness had,
And so-stunned him with wealth that at last he went mad,
And a summersault turned like an acrobat rare,
And his breech broke the leg of St. Peter's gilt chair;
Then he left him and round among monkeries went,
And crammed them with gold till his five years were spent.
And monks fat and idle, and friars white and grey,
Got their wealth from this source—"from the people?" not they!

Then back he returned to his cobbler's stall
And took up his lapstone, sole, hammer and awl;
Was banging away when Old Nick re-appeared,
And growled, "You have spent well my money I've heard,
To give the priests *all* did I save thee from toil,
But for quits I will give thee an extra broil!"

"Show the bond that I gave thee!" bold Crispin replied,
And the sole from his hand at his red nose he shied,
"Thou art Jewed soot-poke thief! for thou'lt see in the scroll,
'Tis spelt *sole*, and not *soul!* Go learn spelling, old fool!"
Old Nick turned blue-black, in a hysteric fit,
And skedaddled at finding the biter was bit.

Then Crispin of Malmsey and Malvoisie drank,
Spelt spelling 'mong spellers in spellers' first rank—
(And cobblers are spellers yet, go where you will,
For proof only look at your cobbler's bill).
He got wed and gave many an abbot a rant,
And the Pope made him canonized, calendar saint,—
And chroniclers holy who can't be denied
Relate that he lived till the day that he died.

A VISION OF JUDGMENT BY A CLAIRVOYANT.

Two judges were throned on two adamant rocks,
In Heaven's Old Bailey, great Calvin and Knox;
    The court crier shouted "O yes,
Has anyone seen in his twistings and turns,
That song-singing sneering shrewd spirit of Burns?
    If he has, bring him forth to confess."

Burns stalked through the crowd and no penitence showed,
And shivered with cold in his clout of a shroud,
    When arraigned at the terrible bar.

"There stands thine accuser," cried snuffling Knox,
" Holy Willie is ready to swear in that box,
   And deny what he says if you dare."

Burns stood and looked round without speaking a word,
When the cries of a batch of young bairnies were heard,
   And Calvin roared "Whence are those brats?"
From Scotland, your Honour." "Then pitch them below,
And shut down the trap, with their squalls as they go,
   Forcordained to be frizzled like rats."

"Bring forward that lout; folk stand out of the way,
You were born to be damn'd, so off with you I say;
   Now, men, what's that screeching about?"
"'Tis his mother," said Knox, "and I trow she's run mad,
She is yelling 'Don't roast my poor innocent lad,'
   Give ear to the mercy besought.'"

"Go, woman," growled Calvin, "Be off and look sharp,
Prithee where hast thou left thy bright crown, robe, and harp,
   No drivelling mercy comes here,
Thou wast born to be saved, and thy son to be damn'd ;
So, hussy, I wonder thou art not asham'd,
   When thou knows't *thou* hast nothing to fear."

Burns stood in amaze, then he fled like a shot
To a place where 'twas neither too cold nor too hot—
   Old Hades and Orcus between,
And grim, holy Willie rushed out with a yell
To bring him to judgment, and wondrous to tell,
Burns gave him the double south-eastward of hell,
   And got tipsy at Fiddler's Green.

THE CHRISTIAN'S VOYAGE OF LIFE.

Shulemah, in the Song of Solomon, 6 c., 13 v., is a Hebrew feminine term, signifying the Church of Christ. See the heading of the chapter.

"Let not the waterflood overflow me; neither let the deep swallow me up, and let not the pit shut her mouth upon me." Ps. 69, 15.

   Black ocean's gulfs are bellowing—hark !
   Euroclydon is hoarsely growling
  Around my feeble shivering bark,
   Like wolves the mighty winds are howling,

Am I forgotten, Shulemah—
My light my hope, my Shulemah?
Hell's legions urge the crested surge
That roars in wild convulsions rolling.

The moon is blood, the black sun hid;
Dark forms of waterspouts are soaring,
Whirl'd on a watery pyramid;
Sulphureous fires are on me pouring.
O light thy beacon, Shulemah!
Thy spirit lode-star, Shulemah!
Storm is behind, and in the wind,
I hear the deadly breakers roaring.

Bilge-water bale, close reef the sail,
Horror reigns dark and dreary;
And see, by phosper-sparkles pale,
Sea monsters glaring near me.
O light thy love star, Shulemah!
Thy star of Bethlehem, Shulemah!
For sore distress'd my sad request,
To live is for the love I bear thee.

The brine flood breaks adown my cheeks,
My cries are down the tempest driven:
Crashing the sudden thunder breaks,
To leeward in the angry heaven.
O hear thy sailor, Shulemah!
Have pity on me, Shulemah!
Wild billows rise and lash the skies,
Mid meteor bolt and blazing levin.

I hear a distant silver bell
Amid the uproar sweetly ringing,
And see among those fires of hell
A steady star's clear light unspringing.
I'm not forsaken, Shulemah!
It is thy beacon, Shulemah!
O'er ocean drear, in radiance clear,
The break of day in purple bringing.

And now thy maidens round me throng,
And now I'm in thy Father's tower!
The *new wine* flows to harp and song,
Thou lead'st me to thy secret bower.
Now since I'm with thee, Shulemah!
Now since thou lov'st me, Shulemah,
I'd brave again the raging main,
Its billows' wrath and tempests' power!

THE RESURRECTION OF SWEDENBORG:

A VISION.

NE FLETO: ECCE VICIT LEO ILLE EX TRIBU JUDA. APOCALYPSIS.

THE passing bell had rung its knell through proud Augusta's
    towers,
And dark Azrael had summed up the Seer of Sweden's hours;
The crown of wisdom's brightest rays shone from his noble
    brow,
And his lineaments celestial wore a robe like driven snow;
A white dove nestled in his breast, a horrid hydra curl'd,
Dead 'neath his feet, as entering the spiritual world.

All radiant as Apollo, when morn's red horizon near,
The blazing chariot roll'd that bore the wondrous charioteer;
Of fiery gold, with living stars and jewels 'twas emboss'd,
And high and terribly their heads his flaming chargers toss'd;
The groves of Eden bent their rosy heads, and from on high
New light appear'd descending like a deluge from the sky.

Like the voice of many waters, when sky lashing surges roll,
All heaven advanced to meet him with a shout from pole to pole;
Standards arose like boreal streamers o'er old ocean's breast,
And in ranks of millions hail'd him, the bright armies of the
    blest!
On either hand with burnish'd shields, like full moons beaming
    free,
The way was lined with serried files, heaven's awful chivalry.

Make way! make way! for Swedenborg—the temple's veil is
    riven—
Angels rejoice, the conqueror comes, the triple crown'd of
    heaven;
To loftier themes than e'er yet heard awake the golden string,
And ye constellations join your songs to the general welcoming:
Awake, ye heavens of heavens, awake, a king approaching see,
Empyrean cherubim, advance, to bear him company!

What news from deep Euphrates? What news from banks of
    Nile?
Stands Memphis yet, or Babylon, as proudly as erewhile?
Does the city of Zenobia all its beauty yet retain?
Are the high Olympic games preserv'd where once flow'd Pindar's
    strain?
Glides bright Eurotas down into the blue Egean sea,
Unsullied yet by tyrant's feet? Is Greece among the free?

What news from old Iberia, and Lisbon's ramparts strong?
Does Gades, or Grenada green yet trill the Moorish song?
Stands Rome yet on her seven hills in high imperial pride?
Sings Florence from her rose bowers to the Adriatic's bride?
How fares it with Helvetia? Do lawless bandits dwell
Yet by the rolling Danube's banks; the Rhine, or the Moselle?

Oh France! oh love! oh troubadours! oh knights who bent the
    knee
To the ladies of the tournament in highborn pageantry!
Has reason yet taught Burgundy the voice of God to hear,
And cast aside the battle axe, or broke the Norman spear?
Lutetia, does she dream of peace, or tune the minstrel's strain?
Oh speak of lovely Provence and the land of Charlemagne.

What tidings from the banks of Clyde? What news from
    Tweed and Ayr?
From Solway, Yarrow, Forth and Dee, and Ettrick's forest
    fair?
What news from crag, and scar, and fell? flies yet the eagle
    free?
Are Stirlings towers standing yet; Dunedin and Dundee?
Is Caledonia yet as proud, or is she great as when
Her claymore flash'd at Bannockburn, over kilted highlandmen?

O tell us of green Erin; is it yet a land of gloom?
Do Romish dupes, our countrymen, retain their ancient home?
Round Tara's halls do yet cold blooded brute assassins dwell?
Does famine o'er her fertile downs uplift its horrent yell?
Or has the emerald land at last retrieved her long disgrace?
Or will her woes end but when ends her bad Milesian race?

Fair England does she conquer still by mighty arm and mind?
Do art and science bless her sons, industrious and kind?
Do bards by Thames and Severn sing? Flows learning's
    lucent tide
From London over every land the boon of thought denied?
Sounds freedom's trumpet still from high Helvellyn's misty
    brow,
To where 'mong sun-lov'd vales and gardens Devon's fountain's
    flow?

Thus as they came they questioned him, and as from mountain
    storm,
Crown'd like an antique runic scald came Ossian's misty form,
With the classic sage of Hawthornden came Scotia's royal
    James;
And Scandinavia's minstrels with their long forgotten names:

Greeting him king Alfred came, old England's royal gem,
Bending his head far flashing with a starry diadem.

With lambent glories round his brow, from Scio's sounding seas
Old Homer came, tower'd Illions bard with all his Hellenes;
There Virgil his bright cohorts led, escaped sublunar woe,
From Tiber, dancing Ticino, and sky blue Anio,
There Milton came who blind on earth, now with the best
    could see,
And with glory Shakespeare rose that drown'd the glories of
    the three.

There Hermes came who tuned Mizraim's mystic Memnian
    lyre,
And Zoroaster, with old Chaldea's worshippers of fire;
Cæsar and Alexander, with their brazen legions bold;
Cyrus and Darius, with their satraps clad in silk and gold;
Epaminondas, Pericles, unto their countries dear—
Sophocles, and Socrates, and Plato too were there.

O marvellously beautiful Helvetia's hero Tell,
Appear'd 'mong freedom's martyred sons the cavalcade to
    swell;
And Wallace now a cherub came in robes of gold and blue,
Avenged of cruel Edward and his faithless country too;
And Cromwell shining still more bright, had lost fanatic gloom,
The leveller of monkeries, the dreaded scourge of Rome.

And there was Aristarchus, who showed the astral way,
To Ptolemy, Copernicus, Galileo, Tycho Brahe;
But Newton, the celestial led the astronomic van,
Type of the boundless Uranos, the more than mortal man;
And kings and princes, bards and heroes, lov'd and great, and
    good,
Unnumbered and unmentioned, swell'd the mighty multitude.

All hail, resounded far and wide, as myriads moved along,
Red lightning wreathed the choiristers that swell'd the soul of
    song;
High as high heavens sublimest reach such harmony they
    raise,
That one soft echo nature vast had silenced and amazed,
Though nature's loudest voice had through her diapason roll'd,
From the hoarse earthquake's deepest groan, to tinkling strings
    of gold.

Careering fiery chariots flamed in radiant array,
And horses clothed with thunder tramp'd along the star pav'd
    way,

And trumpet call'd to trumpet; as their reveilles long they
    blew,
And thunder talk'd with thunder as triumphantly they flew;
And music sounding from afar, with answering music strove,
For joy in treble concord join'd the tenor strain of love.

He comes, the lion conqueror, upon his shoulder borne
The mystic golden key that ope's the pearly gates of morn;
(The New Jerusalem long closed) Like the dread tornado's roll,
Hosannahs shook the trembling spheres, and woke each distant
    pole;
Sinai's trumpet's voice again through heaven rung loud and long,
And millions entering through the open portal, raised the song.

SONG.

Immanuel, thy land is fair, thy rivers flow with wine;
Thine olives and pomegranates bloom, and Sharon's roses
    shine;
All silver-wing'd, thy turtles coo, flowers 'neath our footsteps
    spring;
Thy living streams with emerald banks, sweet things are mur-
    muring:
Bring forth the harp, the organ bring, the viol and the lute,
' Tis our Passover—the trumpet now shall never more be mute.

We've thrown off Egypt's burden's—left her locust eaten
    plains—
Her iron furnace we've escaped, and burst her brazen chains;
The burning desert we have pass'd and weary was the way,
And we know we sinned in murmuring in many a bitter day;
Come forth ye virgins to the dance, with cymbal, pipe and
    lute,
'Tis our Passover—the trumpet now shall never more be mute.

Jehovah walk'd in fire before, and Jordan's waters fled,
As proudly o'er his banks he flowed, and swell'd upon his bed;
The Canaanite beheld our tribes with sad and troubled brow,
And Giants that withstood our march dissolved like summer
    snow:
Come forth, ye sons of Israel, ye children of the blest,
For the trumpet of the Passover, shall henceforth know no
    rest.

Howl in your temples Baal's sons, for Mammon raise the cry,
For wing'd destruction coming fast, and storm and tempest
    nigh,
Leviathan with hooks is caught, (a laughter for the crowd,)
Our children with the monster play, (the king of all the proud;)

The heathen's land is chang'd to pitch, and burns where
   ravens dwell,
While the Passover we keep in thy green land, Immanuel.

Now the silver moon shall never set, the sun shall ne'er decline,
And cloudless constellations sing for ever as they shine;
Unfurl love' banners to the breeze, shout over mount and main,
For righteousness and peace have kiss'd—they'll never part
   again;
Heaven's windows open wider still, louder the clarions swell,
For the Passover we keep in thy green land, Immanuel.

Our Zion's girt with mountains, and her towers ascend the
   sky,
Her citizens are monarchs, crown'd with awful majesty;
Through Salem's golden streets they dance, and in her bower's
   rest,
And banquet on the fruits of life, still day by day more blest;
O never more against her king in thought can they rebel,
For the Passover they keep in thy green land, Immanuel.

A JUBILEE FOR THE GOLDEN AGE.

To HENRY GRATTAN, ESQ.

"And I heard as it were the voice of a great multitude, and as the
voice of many waters, and as the voice of mighty thunderings, saying
Alleluia; for the Lord God omnipotent reigneth." Rev. xix, 6.

ANGELIC Mazzaroth of flame in Canaan's sapphire skies,
Arcturus's burning sons of song, and Eden's Pleiads, rise!
The bearer of the gospel comes from Paran's mystic height,
His face is Salem's sabbath sun, his raiment is its light.
From Dan to Beersheba arise! He comes from Galilee,
The Father, Hero, King of Kings! Meet him with jubilee.

The stone has sunk deep in the brow of Anak's giant son,
From Siloa's brook and David's sling that stone deliverance
   won.
Astræa comes with jewelled hand to shed her sweets divine,
And balmy Gilead, Olivet, and Carmel, bloom and shine;
Grape clusters from the heavens hang to all the nations free,
From that one Vine whence flows new wine that cheers our
   jubilee.

The Sun of Love stands still at last o'er Gibeon's mountains
   blue,
The mountains of our fatherland that glimmer with the dew;

The mystic dew of Hermon falls on leaves that never fade,
And cold Astarte's planet wanes o'er Ajalon delay'd :
The tree of life o'ershades the earth (the prophet's mystic tree.)
And underneath man, beast, and bird. hold happy jubilee.
Philistia hears our Alleluias, bending feeble bow,
And Babel's dragon-god foresees impending overthrow.
Many crowns our Monarch wears—grasps Judah's sceptre
    dread—
Rides on Elijah's chariot by his royal cherubs sped.
He comes to reign for evermore ! sound shalm and psaltery !
For in our bright pavilions He has join'd our jubilee !

CHRISTMAS CAROL.

——:o:——

Bring hither boys the holly bough
With berries bright and red ;
The ivy from the ruined tower,
Where owls shriek o'er the dead ;
The misletoe with mystic power ;
And winter's garland weave,
And the yule logs blaze shall shed its rays,
To cheer our Christmas eve.

The rack rides fast, deep howls the blast,
Where is the linnet now ?
And where the rose of sunny June ?
The blossoms of the sloe ?
They're gone but they'll return again ;
And meantime lest we grieve,
We'll warm our hearts with wassail cups,
And cheer cold Christmas eve.

Come Betty dear—no voice of love
In nature now we hear—
But angels near us whisper it
Through all the varied year.
In cold or heat, in gloom or shine,
The heart it shall not leave,
For as when sultry summer reigns,
It burns at Christmas eve.

We'll wake the viol's merry strings,
While tempest clouds advance ;
And while the pane cracks with big hail,
We'll tread the careless dance.

Thus shall the souls warm summer shine,
Till changeful earth we leave;
And the yule fire and the wassail bowl,
Shall cheer our Christmas eve.

THE TRIAL AND SENTENCE OF THE NIGHTINGALE.

A FABLE.

REPLETE with envy, scorn, and hate,
From hill and dale in lone retreat,
  Gather'd once on a time,
A court of birds to judge in state
The nightingale—and what his fate
  The Muse shall give in rhyme.

In court perch'd not one friendly bird,
No plea was for the culprit heard,
  For judge and plaintiff too
Was each, and hubbubs round were raised,
Of accusations that amazed,
  Philomel cowering low.

First spoke the eagle, reverenced he
Amongst the aristocracy,
  Of fowls for lordly sway,
He looked down on each democrat
And claw'd him whether lean or fat,
  Whene'er he wanted prey.

That wretch quoth he, the whole night long,
Keeps up a never wearied song,
  And wakes me on the rock;
His ways are so unlike my own,
His rustic manners, mind and tone,
  Would any eagle shock.

He ceased, and then upspoke the owl,
I hate his music in my soul,
  I hoot and so should he;
I scream chim'd in the flippant jay,
Quake, quake, says duck, is what I say,
  And this day quake shall he.

Why cant he chatter shriek'd the pies,
Or cheerily chirrup sparrow cries,

O

Says dove he ought to coo ;
Cuckoo screams cuckoo is most fit,
Quoth chanticleer, all birds of wit
   Shout cock-a-doodle-doo.

Why ask'd the rook cant he cry caw,
And why not jack sneer'd grey poll'd daw,
   Sure chirp'd the thrush he's blind ;
Said lark he sings to low for me,
And all agreed he ne'er could bo
   A bird of any mind.

So with redbreast, redstart, and wren
Finch, ouzle, linnet, dacre-hen,
   Having defence denied ;
The birds condemned him one and all,
And on him each began to fall,
   And peck him till he died

MORAL.

Fools would command and compel others too,
To think as they think, and to do as they do.

DAVY AND NANCY; OR, FILIAL OBEDIENCE REWARDED.

BLUSHING crimson, like the even
   Ere the sun-ray leaves the sky,
Davy met his lovely Nancy
   'Mong Ben Rhydding's rustling rye :
" Wilt thou stay and listen, dearest,
   To a lover's tale of woe,
While the corncrake's mate is calling ?"
   Nancy sweetly answered, " No."

" Wherefore dost thou scorn me, loved one ?
   Tell me while there's no one nigh,
Ere the linnet ceases singing
   'Mong the breezy rolling rye.
Fain the fate that lies before me
   From thy ruby lips I'd know ;
May I live and live to love thee ?"
   Nancy faintly answered, " No."

"Hard thine heart, thou cruel maiden,
   Time and tide may now go by ;

Never more I'll wield the sickle
  'Mong the wildly waving rye.
Stay, yet stay, and hear mine anguish,
  See the tear unbidden flow !
Would'st thou see me pine and languish ?"
  Nancy, trembling, answered, "No."

" Why, then, dost thou pain me, Nancy ?"
  The moon o'er Rowley woods rides high ;
Tell me or thou shalt not leave me
  Till her light has left the rye !"
" Davy, then, the truth I'll tell thee—
  Promise but to let me go,—
To a lover's questions, mother
  Bade me always answer ' No !' "

Stars may blink and corn may rustle,
  Dew may varnish poppies' dye,
For a thousand years a-coming
  O'er Ben Rhydding's rolling rye ;
But no happier wedded couple
  Will approving angels bless,
For to her mother true was Nancy
  Till she bade her answer " Yes."

A VISION OF DEATH.

I fa man keep My saying he shall never see death.—John, 8, 61.

At dead of night, when Luna shone
Cold, still, and blue o'er Bradford town,
And still the lurries roar,
I lay in lone and sleepless pain,
And mused on life—so short and vain—
And friends long gone to come again
And cheer me never more.

Then, with a groan, I turn'd my head,
And saw a form beside my bed—
A putrid thing, sans life and soul,
With sightless gaze and visage foul—
Wrapp'd in a mouldy shroud.
Pray, what art thou, in fun'ral cowl ?
I asked.   Art from some graveyard stole ?
Dost think to scare somebody, fool,
That thou art now abroad ?

I'm death, he answered; ha! ha! ho!
My charnel visage dost not know?
Dost mark me? Ha! ha! ho?
Dost laugh? I cried. With thy sad face
I think thy mirth is out of place!
But, come, unfold thy mission here,
Thou that so seldom bring'st good cheer—
Why left thy coffin now?

Ha! ha! ha! Art not afraid
Thy turn so nigh for tomb and shade?
Ho! curdles not thy blood?
Why, bless thee Death, no stranger thou;
I've twigg'd thy phiz long, long ago;
Dos't deem me craven-hearted now,
Thou com'st with laughter rude.

Ha! ha! ha! He's not afraid,
I heard in shouts like music said;
Then Death perform thy task!
And casting off his death's head raw,
Grave clothes and bloody bones, I saw
A spirit (as Orion bright,
With starry baldrick in the night)
Had worn the horrid mask.

Who art thou, glorious being, tell?
My name he sang, is Azrael,
By Milton doem'd the birth of hell!
And round the world I range.
I smite the guilty soul with fear,
But oft unmask—the good to cheer,
With transformation strange.

Heaven, while he spoke, around him glow'd;
Again a shout of laughter loud
And a voice cried from the radiant crowd
To christians Azrael,
No ghost is seen with vizor grim—
Away ye blue-eyed cherubim!
Ha! ha! ha! and all grew dim;
And the spirit-curtain fell.

LIMBO: A MYSTERY IN TWO SCENES.

Scene First—NERO (SOLUS).

Enee! but I am well rewarded now,
I've fish'd and lash'd the murky Stygian lake

(Since Satan and I turn'd papists)—seventeen centuries
As ghosts bring computation from the earth,
And lately caught but minnows, paltry schisms,
Food suitable to rabble imps and fogey gnomes;
Mehercule! but now I'll have a feast,
Th' archfiend shall be invited to the treat,
My fiddlestick I'll rosin well and play
The merry tune I play'd to burning Rome.

Enter FLIBBERTIGIBBET.

What smug and impudent spirit art thou?

FLIBBERTIGIBBET.

I am hell's lamplighter. 'Tis I who clean and feed,
Its myriad glims with naptha from the Styx.

NERO.

Sirrah, hast seen king Sathanas of late?

FLIBBERTIGIBBET.

But now I saw his flaming chariot roll
Through Atraogorgon, from a visit brief,
To Italy, the Pope to aid in th' Œcumenical councils'
Inauguration; and antiquated blasphemies
To fulminate 'gainst powers divine and human.

NERO.

Then, bat-winged varlet, be my messenger,
And tell his grisly majesty from me,
That angling in the lake with bait of gold,
A fish I hook'd, I think of genus shark
To naturalists unknown, and I name "Ritualism"—
Its dorsal fin a bristling row of candles—
Also convey that I his duteous servant,
Request him here with all his court to grace
My banquet, which will be ready at ravin time,
In my poor house in High Church square.

Scene Second. THE BANQUET.

Satan, Nero, Popes, Primates, and Priests discovered.

SATAN.

Henchman, fill our royal goblet reaming full
Of blood and sweat! 'Tis of an ancient vintage,
Crusted and racy. Mighty Hierophants
Will you take it neat or mix'd,

OMNES.

Mixed, your majesty.

NERO.

Take a little more Ritualism most august peers,
'Tis stuffed and spiced in Popery fashion,
Its flavour I think exceeds that standing dish,
Of gulls and bedlamites.
        Satan, (taking his cup),
            In troth 'tis excellent Nero.

Fiends, Popes, Primates, powers ecclesiastical —
Members of the guilds of pride, avarice, falsehood,
Presumption and blasphemy, fill your cups,
A health to one to whom we are indebted
For this new dainty feast Lucullian
I need not mention " Pusey !"
    All rising—A health to Dr. Pusey. (cheers)

SONG.

Let Rome fill up Belshazzar's cup,
  The toast we honour all ;
Let rituals speed and fools go read
  Hand writings on the wall.

The ears of heaven are ever closed
  To soul's in prisons cries,
And Laic Dupes of Clergic knaves,
  Still love their enemies.

High rears his hood the serpent dread,
  As when the world began ;
The time is past to bruise his head,
  He fears no Son of Man.

LARRY AND BIDDY.

——:o:——

" OICKS, open the door, mabouchal, me honey !
  I've thramped through the moss, and I'm wary and wake ;
I will die wid the frost, purty Biddy O'Roony—
  And ye shure wad not wish me to die for your sake.
Be jabers an' 'ouns ! 'tis a keen blasht, I tell ye ;
  An' the hot love will roasht me poor heart, I am shure ;

An' I shware be saint Bride's holy tongs of Molkelly,
    Wid me bit o'shillalah I'll batther your door."

"Och, Larry, ye spalpeen! go now, an' be asy;
    Will I open the door, thin, and let out the hog,
The son o' yer mother musht think I am crazy;
    I wisht in me heart ye were smoor'd in the bog.
Larry O'Keefe, if yer love is so warram,
    Set yer brogues a bog-throttin an bother no more ;
Or shtand in the cold, that will do yez no harram,
    For I tell yez at wanst I'll not open the door."

"But, Biddy O'Roony, jist now, whilst I'm spakin',
    I thrimble wid wet, and I thrimble for you :
And I'm kilt dead wid grief, and me poor heart is brakin',
    Will yez come to me wake, hoo, ochone, pillilew !
I will go to Peg Brennan, an' tell her me throuble,
    And throuble my Biddy O'Roony no more ;
I will tell her wid love I am nearly bint double,
    And at wanst she'll get up an' throw open her door."

"Ish't of Peg that ye spake? Durty wather upon her,
    She shtrides wid a limp, and she shtares wid a shquint
Go to her ! Why I'd die or go hang meself sooner,
    Larry, acoushla come now be contint.
Och, murther, avick, I wid me feelins yere spoortin'.
    Come in for thares potheen an' praties galore—
Musht I tell yez whinever a boy goes a coortin',
    He should always thry furst can he open the door.!

THE FORCE OF EXAMPLE.

—:o:—

"Hieland Willie gang thy way,"
    I said ae bonnie e'enin':
I might as weel hae bade him stay,
    I trow he guess'd my meanin'.

Our auld sheep collie kens him weel
    By many a kindly token,
An' to the spence will let him steal,
    An' mither winna wauken.

I'll no bide, I canna bide,
    I winnna bide sic suing,
Wi' warsling love he wearies me,
    My heart' sair wi' wooing!

Out ower the hills he gaily bangs
    When sheep and kye are stelling,
And far awa I hear his sangs
    Sound frae his shepherd sheiling.

I canna wander down the brae
    Though ere sae fause an' warie,
But up he starts frae broom or slae
    And laughs when I am eerie.

I stole awa beyont the shaw
    A day to see my auntie,
And ere I got to Cragielaw
    He met me blithe and jauntie.

Meg Allen's wed, an' night an' day
    There's ne'er a ane to tent her;
I met her wet and clogg'd wi' clay,
    An' nane I saw behint her.

She gaed ae night athwart the lea
    Wi' neither moon nor starnie,
An' her guid man ne'er came to see
    Gin she fell in the burnie.

They say that Willie loes me weel,
    Is leal, kind, and canny—
An' troth I think sae to mysel,
    But daurna tell't to any.

An' I've a scheme I'll whisper none,
    An' soon I'll fairly fit him,
I'll gang and do as Meg as done—
    An' wed him just to quit him!

THE MILLENNIUM.

A Song in Correspondences.

("The desert shall blossom as the rose."—Isa. xxxv. 1.

The dark bitter winter of death shall depart,
And the season of song shall return to the heart;
'Neath the fig tree and vine the beloved shall dwell,
And the voice of the turtle bid sorrow farewell;
And the day-star of Bethlehem for ever shall shine
With a radiance unclouded—the Presence Divine!

No more o'er the olive siroccos shall blow,
The vintage shall redden, the wine vat o'er flow ;
Joy shall sit on the throne of the sorrow of yore,
And terrors and tears will be heard of no more ;
For the star of the Magi in th' Orient shall shine
With a beauty eternal—the Presence Divine.

No more from the thicket the wolf shall destroy,
Nor the fox in his covert his cunning employ,
No grim hungry lion for ravin will roar,
 The flocks and the herds shrink and shiver no more—
For the day-star of love, for the Presence Divine,
The perfection of beauty for ever will shine.

In the salt sultry desert sweet fountains shall play,
And the wilderness blossom in rosy array ;
Where the dark venomed weeds hid the snake in their
    gloom,
Shall Pomona bring fruits in the day of her bloom ;
For the day-star eternal, the Presence Divine,
In th' expansion, his mansion, for ever shall shine !

The clash of the falchion, the rush of the steed,
The hurrahs of armies, the phalanx's tread,
Shall cease—and the voice of the trumpet be dumb,
And the harp shall be sounded instead of the drum,
And Urania's bright sons veiled with glory shall shine,
Hymning—Blest be the star of the Presence Divine !

The red field of strife shall be jocund and blithe,
And the sword shall be bent into sickle and scythe :
The plough for the spear, and the wain for the car,
Shall be seen in the fields of the carnage of war,
And the veil will be rent, and the Visage Divine
(So marred) in its beauty for ever shall shine !

ADAM'S METAMORPHOSIS.

——:o:——

MELANCHOLY and lonely sat Adam and Eve,
Deploring a loss they could never retrieve ;
The red threat'ning brands of the Cherubs shone forth
O'er the gate like the meteor streams of the north ;
And the winds sigh'd and sobb'd in the fig tree above
The couch of the exiles of Eden and Love,

A stranger appeared. Arm'd and regal his form,
Like rider and ruler of ruin and storm;
In the flash of his eye evil principles blazed;
With the war bolts of heaven his forehead was grazed;
His voice like the earthquake was heavy and dull,
Or the low moan of Thetis when hurricanes lull.

" Why weep ye, poor children, for Paradise lost?
Why linger and gaze on yon pitiless host?
Archangelic—a god—heaven rings with my fame.
Earth is given to me; and Apollyon my name.
Rejoice! for a Paradise happy and new
You shall enter by drinking nepenthè I brew."

Mute they sat, as a calabash near him he seized
And filled to the brim from vine clusters he squeezed:
" Let the sun kiss it thrice in his race of the day,
The moon kiss it twice with her starry array;
Then drink without stint ! It will open your eyes
To Edens that angels will view with suprise!

Father Adam drank first and he danced on the sod,
He felt as a monarch and spoke like a god;
And Eve looking on in his marvellous feast
Beheld him transform'd to a Satyr-like beast;
And his presence she fled with affright at the change
Lest her form should be turn'd into something as strange.

The sky became bronze, like the advent of doom,
The Cherubs of Eden more fierce in the gloom;
The pit oped its jaws with that fire unhallow'd,
First offer'd to God by false Korah, (earth swallow'd,)
And horrors unnumber'd on earth came to reign,
Magicians can never exorcise again.

Eve again sought her mate, through her tears in the morn,
And there he lay writhing and groaning and 'lorn;
His shape had return'd, but the Harpies of hell
Were tearing his vitals with laughter and yell:
They fled her approach, and Apollyon since then
With Edens has cheated and brutalized men.

MY FIRST RAILWAY TRIP FROM BRADFORD TO LEEDS.

———:0:———

Each silently musing upon this vocation,
Sat down in his carriage at Bradford's grand station,

When the steam began harshly to snort, hiss and yell,
And then mov'd with a clash rather slowly and wearily,
Gaining in speed till we gallop'd right merrily,
Flying at length with such speed that I verily
Thought we had mounted the chariot of hell.

The houses 'gan dancing with wonderful capers,
The pollar'd oaks waltzed in the blue mists and vapours,
The sky like a whirligig wheel'd overhead,
The stormy wind rose as when witches are dying,
As faster and faster in showers of fire flying,
And thunders to rumble their deepest bass trying,
Down trembling and echoing Airedale we sped.

With crashes like bombs bursting round us to shivers,
We shot under bridges, o'er meadows and rivers,
Through deep dismal bowels of mountains we dash,
There Erebus thickened in horrors confounded,
As if Etnean Cyclops their anvils had sounded
Earth's knell to the gods as the hills go to smash.

Like the hurricanes demon that drives o'er dark waters,
And the billows white crests like the winter snow scatters,
And shatters tall ships in his ruinous route ;
When waterspouts dismal, in whirlwinds are soaring,
And riding the tempest the hailcloud is snoring,
And mermaids look out on the wilderness roaring,
And wonder what such a commotion's about.

Like the furious and mad mountain cataract dashing,
Over beetling crags curling, boiling and flashing,
Like a star blink, a bullet, a dart, or a thought,
Like Mars when he rides over black desolations,
Or red hairy comets when wide conflagrations,
They spit in huge meteors to frighten the nations,
We rode into Leeds and stood still and got out.

THE SCOTCH PACKMAN'S LOVE LETTER.

—— :o: ——

'Tis gloomy Yule-tide, Maggie dear,
The sun blinks coldly frae the lift ;
Hoarse hurtling blasts the welkin tear,
I stumble through the frozen drift,
My heart is wae in Southland clime
When I remember happy days,

The glints o' love in simmer's prime,
And we our lane on Logan braes.

Forget me not for a' for thee
My weary pack I daily bear ;
And biding what my wierd may be
Through storm and shine I stoutly steer.
Thy love as Scotland's star is true
That sailors guide in danger's ways,
Thine eyes o' blue were dim wi' dew
When last we met on Logan braes.

The pickle siller that I get
I count at night to ae bawbee,
And hoard wi' care, for nearer yet,
And nearer steps are they to thee.
My heart to care and toil I nerve,
And bide the brunt o' weary days,
For joy and siller I reserve,
For thee and bonny Logan braes.

Still keep thy heart aboon sweet lass,
We'll yet stock mailen ha' and yaird,
And many a happy yule we'll pass,
And ye'll be canty wi' your laird
We'll tent our lambs and bairnies blest,
Where langest rosy simmer stays,
When I return to thee and rest
And love and home on Logan braes.

OLD MRS. BULL'S MEDIATION BETWEEN PRUSSIAN BILL AND FRENCH NAP.

—:o:—

Says Mrs. Victoria, be ruled my dear Bill,
Curb your temper; don't fight, psha, says Bill but I will.
Do you think I'll be bullied by insolent Nap,
When I've just fought and humbled as clever a chap ;
Gott's blitzen and hagel, I see your intention,
Mediation from you is concealed intervention.

So, so ; old Herr Spitfire, But here with a swagger
Comes Nap with his moustache, with point like a dagger,
Dear, faithful ally, sure you know how I love you ;
Why allow Sigmaringen so strangely to move you ?

Spain's Prim is a villain for hawking it's crown,
Too thorny to wear, or he'd make it his own.

Remember your uncle, for victories famed,
He fought till he got both imprisoned and lamed;
Let bygones be bygones, you are now high in station,
Don't quarrel for faults of a past generation,
Mind your home affairs, Monseur, and later or sooner
The world will award you your just due of honour.

Who knows, but your crown some bold knave may be hawking
Some months hence—Quoth Nap, it is useless you talking,
Sacre diablo, madame, I'll show Bill this day
How honour is won, in a *coup d'etat* way,
So be silent, old girl, if a snub you'd escape,
Mediators oft get themselves into a scrape.

Dear me, sigh'd poor Vic; did you ever, no never;
Lackaday! Parlous speaking to persons so clever,
I wish to a halter's two ends you were strung,
Each hanging himself while the other is hung.
-But I'll home and warn John, while I'm darning his stocking,
To keep out of quarrels so foolish and shocking.

ISABEL AND NORA.

Nor.—DEAR ISABEL, why dost thou stay
    Frae hame sae late at e'en?
Thy mither flytes thee day by day,
    And speers where thou hast been.

Isa.—I carena for my mither's frown;
    I love the gloaming lea,
And a ramble with the witching moon
    On primrose braes for me!

Nor.—But sister awesome bogles glare,
    And cantrips oft are laid—
O' gloaming dean and shaw beware,
    They've ruined many a maid.

Isa.—Though bogles grin in grisly ranks,
    I wadna eerie be;
And the wicken shaw by Ettrick's banks
    And Ettrick's sough for me!

Nor.—But Ettrick's streams are false they say,
    When glint the starry skies;

And wandering footsteps will betray,
    When mists of midnight rise.

Isa.—Hadst thou e'er known the pleasures lone
    Beneath the greenwood tree,
And conversed with the spaewife moon
    Thou wouldst not plead with me !

A nuptial passed the brownie knowe,
    Ere leaves of autumn fell ;
And bonny lassies whispered low,
    The bride is Isabel.

And still she sang, I love the lone
    Dim shades of glen and lea,
And a stolen ramble with the moon
    On Ettrick's banks for me !

TO NAPOLEON III.

——:o:——

NAPOLEON THE THIRD, thou wert well with thy mask on,
Thy Plebiscite, army, and flunkey, and Gascon,
Thou wert throned 'mong the gods, and thy dictum was fate,
Thy will was a nation's, thy person the State ;
And thou would play at war's bagatelle. Wager thy throne,
And art learning with sorrow to let *well* alone.

Thou would'st baptize thy son unto Moloch in fire,
Father inhuman thou hadst thy desire ;
But "vaulting ambition" perchance had forgot
That the baptismal font might be rather too hot,
That the fire-king of battles is often uncivil,
And a long spoon is best when we sup with the Devil.

Was it "peace" with French sages and patriots banished,
When the organs of reason and liberty vanished.
Was the *coup d'etat* peace, the Republic trod down
In exile and blood in thy greed for a crown ;
Colossus of fear that Republic from shame
And death hath arisen a Phœnix from flame ;

The nightmare Imperial, the bugbear, the scorn
Of Europe is seen in the blaze of its morn.
Thou didst petrify nations around with a glance,
But "Unity" laughed at the gorgon of France ;

And thy prestige's vanity raving with spite
Breath'd death while still flaunting false banners of white,
And thou rushed like a brigand run mad to thy doom;
Eldest son, hated shield of infallible (?) Rome!

Napoleon! Thy crown for the foolscap of fame
Thou hast bartered. Go wear it in bondage and shame,
Learn France that thy glory and honour shall shine
Yet again; but the terrible cost shall be thine,
And the brute's lesson learn that delight in a fray,
That war is a game at which angels can play;
That battle fiends must and soon will be chain'd down
With the dragon who never could let *well* alone.

VISION OF A NORSELAND GEISTKENNAR

——:o:——

The Druid harper's gaze was rivetted with amaze,
  On a visionary battle-field afar,
And he heard from blue Moselle, trumpet blare and clangour
  swell,
  From the tocsin of the demonry of war.

Scandinavia's Thor divine, from the Baltic to the Rhine
  He heard from grim Valhalla's temple roar,
Vandal, Visigoth, and Hun, at the dreadful summons run
  To his tournament and revelry of gore.

Dark-visaged braves, bore down from Bavarian mountains
  brown,
  Herculean Hessian yagers led the van,
As royal William's call, rung from Berlin's banner'd wall,—
  " Up my Teutons, up my dragons, every man !

The star of Brunswick's ray show'd the Hanoverian way;
  Bright Polish spears left Scythia's forest gloom,
And the Saxon sabre's clank, toll'd the death knell of the
  Frank,
  While the landsturm drove the engin'ry of doom.

Mighty Odin o'er the Maine, roll'd through hissing missile rain,
  And Oder, Sheldt, and Maes heard the cry
As the ironclad was riven and its shivers cumber'd heaven,
  While the brawny Goth and Teuton's God went by.

Smitten Gallic corses glare on the gleaming earth and air ;
  Their faces in the iron furnace wan,

As royal William's call, rung from Berlin's banner'd wall,—
" Up my Teutons, up my dragons, every man!"

Hark, the moanings of the Seine,' where high festival has
    been,
  The Dying eagle floats to Zuyder Zee,
The Frankish chief in dread, flies the ruin o'er his head,
  And old Germany, the father-land, is free.

The Scalds of olden time heard the prophet's Runic rhyme,
  And, in their Bothnian storms, took up the strain ;
The Druid ceased his song, but his harp rung loud and long,
  As if wailing, sadly wailing, for the slain.

THE OFFERING.

The Empress presented a candle at the church of Notre Dame des
Victoires, for the success of the Emperor's expedition.—*Newspapers.*

ROUND architrave and pilaster, groin'd arch and peristyle,
From dome to hollow sepulchre, through holy Mary's pile,
The organ's miserere roll'd. The priests arrang'd in line
Beheld the Empress humbly seek the Victress Mary's shrine.
Dark Nubian pages bore her train of priceless cramourie.
And a gold and crimson hassock swell'd beneath the royal
  knee.
" Most holy image, heaven's queen, give ear unto my prayer.
My spouse with great M'Mahon rides to glory and to war,
Thou know'st, good image, that his blood is stagnant grown
  and chill,
And doctors say 'twill do him good a little blood to spill.
Restrain him, lest the Prussians all he swallow in his ire;
King, Queen, and royal family, and set the Rhine on fire.
Be gracious, queen of victory, dear image on him smile,
And bless my votive offering thy vigils to beguile."
Thus praying with her jewell'd hand she fumbled in her gown,
Drew forth a pyx, and on the altar laid a candle down ;
Then ambling like the bride of Jove, in heaven's select array,
When Hebe blushed and Pallas smiled, she grandly swept
  away.
The church doors were barred, and the Sacristan gone
To taste his Marne trout, and Madeira alone—
The candle was burning when cross as a wasp
Wooden Mary addressed with a voice like a rasp
A big wooden Christ at his last wooden grasp.
" Sob, we're nobody now, why a nice golden cup

I expected for holy pump-water to sup;
Or a bright diamond ring or a necklace of pearl,
And a candle behold that would shame a street girl.
Cheap worship I trow! marry quip and come up—
But mark me, my lady, thy canter I'll stop,
An Empress forsooth she must come to my shrine,
And insult me a wooden Madonna divine.
My dear wooden Christ turn thy face up and see
An Empress's gift to a lady like me."
And her wooden son laughed with a dull wooden sound,
And the marble saints echoed his laughter around;
And a hundred brass angels with voices sonorous
Cried "Shame" from the pillars and rafters in chorus,
Till Mary glared round with her fierce eyes of glass
And kicked down the candle.   The monks came to mass
In the morning, and out came the pious church scandal
Of the wooden immaculate virgin and candle.

THE MARRIAGE OF TRUTH AND LOVE.

——:o:——

It was Truth and Love went forth one day,
  When Lebanon yet was young;
And Love was sweet, and Truth was gay,
  And the sky with rainbows hung.
And ranging through th' enchanted woods,
  And Eden's holiday lea—
Over the hills and over the floods,
  They met with young Harmonie.

" Where art thou going, thou pretty, pretty youth,
  In thy clerky gown," said they.
" Take out thy book, thy book so sooth,
  And we will be married to-day."
Then out his book he merrily took,
  And married them under Life's tree ;
And voices came forth from heaven and earth
  With " Amens" to Harmonie.

And after his blessing they bent their way
  To higher and grander spheres ;
And angels and men he has married since then
  For many a thousand years.
He has married the light with the ambient air,
  He has married the land and the sea

D

With the astral choirs; and woe to the pair
    Unmarried by Harmonie.

~~~~~~~~~~~~~~~~~~~~~~~~~~~~~~~

BISHOP BLAIZE: HIS GHOST.

——:o:——

At midnight, as lying in silence alone,
    Lost in deep, sleepless thought on my bed,
I heard my name called in sepulchral tone,
    And a light round my chamber was shed ;

And a form with a fadge on its back I espied,
    Clothed in prelatic mitre and stole,
With a wool-comb and oil-bottle held by its side,
    A remarkable ghost on the whole.

" What art thou ?" I sung out, not a little in dread,
    " So untimely, thy business what ?"
"I am Blaize, the Lord Bishop," he solemnly said,
    " The clerical, primitive ' scrat."

" Then you're pulling the tup by the caudal part yet ?—
    Have you got a good dozen, Lord Blaize ?
Is Shakespeare in Spectredom, jigging a bit?
    Are you mates—or he's writing more plays ?

" Have you weighed out a lather?   You're weary I see,
    There have been better days with us both."
He answered, " Quiz not, quondam comber, and be
    Not so free with a ghost of my cloth.

" Of thee and of Bradford I've long been the friend,
    And I come from the shades to deplore
My name in oblivion—my craft at an end—
    Ere I visit the moonlight no more.

" The donkey's death-bray for the comber is gone,
    And the old pot-of-four, once a glow,
Is extinct —gone to pot—the strong padpost pull'd down
    And the comb-shop is desolate now.

" Woe is me, for my annual pageant and fete,
    When my woolcombers, greasy and pale,
Kneaded mud in procession ! Ah, Bradford ingrate—
    Ah, the speeches, the dinners, the ale !

" Things are changed," I replied, " You're a fool to
      complain,
    The arts have progressed since your day."

With the ghost of a tear, then the ghost in disdain
Sighed, and turned in a tantrum away.

Deeply pitying the spectre, I asked, " Is that all
You've to say ere you go, reverend ghost ?
But he hitched up his fadge and walked straight through
the wall,
And my chamber in darkness was lost.

THE KNIGHT OF THE THIMBLE.

——:o:——

THE knight of the thimble at midnight alone,
Went through the thick wood by the light of the moon;
His courage was flush, and enormous his pluck,
Misfortune he dared, and its cousin, ill luck,
And all for young Dowsabel, freckled and fair,
His princess enchanted, with carrotty hair.

The forest was dark, but he cared not a rush,
With some dragon or giant he longed for a brush ;
He tightened his belt, and his sleeveboard he took,
And he brandished his goose with a terrible look ;
As a knight of the thimble the worst he would dare
For the widow bewitched, with the carrotty hair.

A form of young beauty before him appeared :
" Ha ! says he " of false furies in forests I've heard ;
Hence, Satan !" he shouted, and marched boldly on ;
But as he approached her the fairy was gone,
And only a moonbeam before him was there,
This champion puissant and *preux chevalier.*

But an uglier form in the bush met his gaze,—
It was black, horned, and gruesome, with ogles ablaze,
His hair stood erect, and his sleeveboarding shield
And his goose he let fall as he stood on the field :
The monster approached a poor innocent cow,
Strayed and lost in the forest, confronted him now.

He took up his goose and his sleeveboard in haste—
By enchantment the monster had changed to a beast ;
" Thou coward enchanter ! thy feints I now see—
Thou fearest my prowess, and I defy thee ;
Of my sleeveboard and goose, wretch, I bid thee beware,
Till I succour the widow with carrotty hair."

The dark horrid forest he passed without scath,
When a form more than human he found in his path ;
It ran as he ran, and it stood as he stood ;
His brain became dizzy, and icy his blood—
He shook and he shivered, but still he rushed on
Till he came to a castle, then fell in a swoon.

A lady came forth, and he suddenly woke :
" What is that ?" gasped he, " there ! " and with boldness he
    spoke,
" 'Tis your shadow," screamed she. " 'Twas a giant," quoth he,
Changed for fear of my goose to a shadow, d'ye see."
So she made him some tea, and his wounds had her care,
This widow bewitched with the carrotty hair.

BEHOLD THE DREAMER COMETH.

Gen. xxxvii. 19.

LIKE Bunyan, the tinker, I found a rude den,
Remote from the strife and collisions of men ;
I am not a Roundhead I own ; but what then ?—
    I can dream ; and I dreamt I was dead
Methought I stood gazing at heaven's closed gate,
'Twixt hope and despair—(a most pitiful state ;)
Resolving at length in this crisis of fate
    To get rid of my terror and dread.

So I piously struck up a hymn, common metre,
When out rush'd St. Joseph, with angry St. Peter ;
The latter exclaiming : " How are you the greater—
    Am I not the Church's solado ?"
Dismiss'd from my post ! (then he made a quick turn,
Lock'd the door) and resumed : " Ere I give up, I'll learn
Both the why's and the wherefore's ; or, mark me, I'll spurn
    Thine orders, my fine camarado.

The Pope, who rules heaven, beyond all dispute,
Hath made me a saint and his patron to boot."
" You're an ass," quoth St. Joseph, the question to moot ;
    So give up your key and your pennies.
Folk oft keep in office too long as you know,
Reform is much needed, so bundle and go ;
Take your rusty old sword, there is mischief below,—
    Genevieve is in tears with St. Denys."

" Not so fast," snapp'd St. Peter, " Do Councils agree
With Cullen and Manning, the Irishry,
That I should be sack'd and so summarily—
   Does the Lateran vote for all this ?"
" Yes ; and Gladstone succeeds unto Henry the eighth,
As *fidei Defensor* by treachery's right."
" Catch the key," then quoth Peter, and cursing with spite,
   He hurl'd it sheer down the abyss.

" Thank you !" they heard from the dungeons agape,
And out came king Lucifer's right royal shape ;
Fast clutching the key (both the saints in a scrape)
   Addressed—quaking Peter in mirth—
" You have let in my subjects by thousands, you knave,
You have fill'd heaven full of my property, slave ;
But I'll ope and shut now, and see well that I have
   All my own be they Pontiff's henceforth."

LOVE.

——:o:——

KEEN bites the snell blast o'er the wild withered brachan,
Cauld whistles the snaw round the crag and the cairn ;
Come ben, my ain jo, though they talk in tho clachan,
To steek thee out noo I'd a wame o' cauld airn.
Come ben, for my auld graining minnie's asleep,
The night it is mirk and the snaw wreath is deep ;
When I heard thy light step, how it gart my heart leap—
I'll bar the door faster when winter's awa.

O tempt na the burn whar the fause kelpie hovers,
As it rows 'neath the hazel in fury and ire ;
But come to my ingle, wha's peat lowe discovers
The eye kindly glinting ; the lad I admire.
Let them talk o' their prudence, wha's love is grown stale,
Let them steek their doors faster whar fickle and frail,
But virtue courts trial like hero in mail,
And aye is found kinder when simmer's awa.

How lanesome and dreary the banks o' the Yarrow,
The mains and the links are a' cheerless and bare,
But the mavis and merle will think o' their sorrow,
Nae mair when the gowans and bluebells appear.
It is then I'll gae down to the brae whar we met,
And the thorn whar we trysted I winna forget ;
Till then I'll unsteek baith my door and my yett,
And shelter my jo while sweet simmer's awa.

The laird o' Todlowrie has braid lands an' bonny,
An' tempts wi' bright gowd and wi' silks that are braw ;
Mair dear are the bright gowden locks o' my Johnny,
Which gar my heart flutter much faster than a'.
At my blue woolsey gown the proud laird aften kecks,
When o' hantles o' gear and o' mailins he speaks,
But dearer to me are my Johnny's grey breeks,
Wi' his plaid row'd around me when simmer's awa.

ST. VALENTINE'S EVE.

——:o:——

In a wide field of azure in ether's far height,
　Near the galaxy's star-spangled way,
Aquarius throned in the zodiac's light
Courts Terra as round in celestial flight
　She worships the Deus of day.

Thither down from cerulean mansions above,
　An annual legion divine
Of angels, with far flaming torches of love,
Rejoicing descend, dormant passions to move,
　And their captain is St. Valentine.

And they hurl their red firebrands all over the earth—
　Over continent, island, and sea—
Into palace and cottage, and great is their mirth,
To hear what lies, vows, and confessions come forth
　From the lips of the bond and the free.

Then the rulers of earth have their visions that night,
　And their subjects have their visions too,
But not of dominion, conquest, or might,
But of love in its glory and burning delight,
　And of troths everlastingly new.

Then the bachelor turns on his comfortless bed,
　And a syllable mutters or two—
As the flames of the angels upon him are shed,
And he smiles in his sleep for he dreams he is wed
　To a maid whom he lov'd long ago.

The miser then dreams he has wedded a mate,
　A wizened old harridan scold,
Who has stolen his money, and broken his pate,
Then changed to a horrible demon in wait
　For his soul and his coffers of gold.

The poet has visions of Paradise gay,
  Where romance can immortals beguile,
Where Apollo he hears on his sun-chords to play,
And Venus respond with Elysian lay
  To the god from her Paphian isle.

The rest of mankind as they slumbering loll,
  When their hearts feel the quickening fire,
Have fancies so silly, and funny, and droll,
Of Peggy, and Moggy, and Molly and Doll,
  That the Muses with laughter perspire.

Then the golden-bill'd ouzel-cock chirps to the moon,
  And the dove nestles close to the dove,
And up in the morning a-pairing they're gone,
And they shake their bright pinions every one,
  Singing " Welcome the season of love!"

SAINT PATRICK.

——:o:——

SAINT PATRICK had banish'd the toads and the snakes,
From the land of potatoes.   Its ditches and brakes
  Never more heard a hiss or a croak.
" Bad cess to yez all!" was his magical word,
And off, helter-skelter, they all disappear'd ;
  Then he fill'd his duddeen for a smoke.

" Arrah, now," said he, smoking, " what next will I do ?
Bedad, I will clear all the Powy's land too,
  And faste wid King Arthur and Queen."
So he sought King O'Brian at Ballynarogue,
Whom he found kilt with colic, and draining a mug
  Of a gallon of whiskey potheen.

" Is't to Wales ye are bound," said O'Brian, " mo boy ?
Take a drop of the crather, your cold to desthroy ;
  Shure, I'll give ye the loan of my plough."
" Is't of ploughs that ye spake ?" quoth St. Patrick irate,
Will your one shtilted plough the deep say navigate ?   -
  Faith, its joking you are wid me now."

" Yer soul now be asy ; leap deftly asthride,
Hold the stilt in your fisht, and the billows you'll ride,—
  'Tis meself that have crossed in an hour."
" Faix," said the saint, " I will thry ;" and he tried,

And he plough'd through the sea, and he plough'd up the
    Clwyd,
  And he plough'd a long mile on the shore.

And ascending the cliffs to Plinlimmon's grey peaks,
Proclamation he made through the land of the leeks,
    For the varmint to crawl out of that.
But he might have spoke Greek, for no venomous rogue
One syllable knew of his Patlandish brogue ;
    So their case he denounc'd to the State.

Then Tavy ap Morgan ap Shenkins ap Rhyl
Call'd the nobles to Moot, and they fashion'd a Bill,
    That school boards forthwith educate.
The reptiles in brogue—in log, bog, fog, and fen,
And the saint for his miracle's power till then,
    Spell-bound and enchanted must wait.

In Snowdon's huge flank is a rose-tinted glade,
And the halls of Cadwallon enchanted in shade,
    Where paladins banquet unseen,
There he stays with the king of the Cymry and court ;
And the songs of Llewellyn make centuries short,
    And prowess and beauty convene.

They have look'd for him long in old Ballynarogue,
But the reptiles learn slowly the grammar of brogue,
    And Patlanders many there be
Who his " double," from Howth of the tempest and snow,
Have seen like the storm-king astraddle his plough,
  Riding back o'er the sea—the salt sea."

A SCOTTISH LEGEND.

——:o:——

Dugald Dhu, Lord Macdonald, rode down by Strathfenian,
  And high waved his plume in the flash of the morn ,
He met in the glen the sweet Rose of Clangillian,
  And shrieks echoed shrilly from Swindenhaugh burn.

O shame to thy sweet-smiling gowans, Strathfenian,
  O shame to the mavis that sang in the thorn ;
For the maiden dishonoured of high-born Clangillian,
  By the claws of the hawk like the cushat is torn !

Death dwelt in the dim-lighted bower of Rosellen,
  There was wailing and tearing of hair that was grey,
The bell from the turret at midnight was knelling,
  There was cursing and clashing of armour till day.

Who kneels by a flower covered bier in Strathfenian?
The comely and noble young chief of Macleod,
O! he tenderly loved the fair maid of Clangillian,
And weeps like a child with his brow in her shroud.

Then furious the gallop of horse through the heather,
Then fearful the beacon that blazed on the fell,
Like the rushing of waters the angry clans gather,
Like the roar of the tempest the shout and the yell!

On, on, like a madman, Macleod is outsallying—
On, on, fierce Clangillian is howling afar—
Like the storm that rolls down from the crown of Shehallion,
The sons of the Gael rush'd down to the war.

There is woe in Strathfenian, but oh! in that hour,
For the clan of Macdonald the claymore is keen;
The far flashing blazes of cottage and tower,
Lit up the red carnage of horses and men.

Fast fell the clansmen, 'mid hacking and hewing,
And shelterless widows were left to their woe;
The halls of Mackdonald were left a black ruin,
And Dugald Dhu's corse fed the raven and crow.

Wild the coronach on braes of Strathfenian,
Wild are the cries o'er the wounded and slain;
No pibroch is heard from the victor Clangillian,
For lovely Rosellen all vengeance is vain.

Macleod sought again the dark keep in Strathfenian;
Wan, weary, and wounded, he rode o'er the heath,
The heart-broken wreck of the crime of a villian;
He sunk in his gore-stiffened tartan in death.

Side by side with Rosellen he sleeps in Strathfenian,
And lovers at gloaming that wander abroad,
Often see near a tomb with his Rose of Clangillian,
The dim weeping shade of the chief of Macleod.

BATTLE OF THE BOYNE.

July 1st, 1690.

" Sir, yonder on his charger white the bold usurper ride,
My falconet now covers him upon the green-hill side,
Speak, sire, and William shall no more be enemy of thine,
Thy heartless son who seeks thy life upon the banks of Boyne."

" Hold ! Fire not now !" cried good King James, and shed a
  silent tear,
" Leave my unnatural son to Heaven, my skilful cannoneer ;
I would not for my country's crown, my ancestor's and mine,
Commit a crime, though in red war, on deeply rolling Boyne.

Beat, beat to arms Drogheda's drums, my royal banner spread,
Ten thousand helmets wave their plumes o'er squadrons dark
  and dread—
Advance !" cried James, " Our cause is good. Trust in my
  right divine,
Strike in for death or victory ! Brave spirits guard the
  Boyne !"

Dutch William on his war-horse sat, and eyed the hills and
  stream,
And round him his bright bravoes flashed, the morning's ruddy
  beam.
" Sed on," roared he, " mein galland men, we tshow dem
  dagdigs feine,
Ride Schomberg mit mein prave tracoons, und dake de foords
  of Boyne !"

From either bank the sulphurous smoke from heavy ordnance
  rose,
And Hamilton the furious Scot, bore down upon his foes ;
Wild clash and clang, and stab and yell, along the charging line,
Proclaimed that death his harvest reaped, and life-blood
  swelled the Boyne.

High over volleying musquetry St. George's ensign flew,
And fearlessly, 'mid whist'ing shot, Ierne's bagpipe blew ;
Ierne's sons, in fiery wrath, their vengeance all combine,
And thundering, burst through the guard of William on the
  Boyne.

Whig William growled a German oath, and spurred his charger
  o'er
The crimson water, driving through the murderous battle roar,
And James beheld, with sinking heart, his sword terrific shine,
As clouds of horsemen followed, dashing madly o'er the Boyne.

Wo, wo, for Erin's warriors ! they fight, they bleed, they die,
Their corses strew the flowery sward, they scorn to turn and fly,
The ruined father and their king sought sheltering France to
  pine,
And mourn Whig rage and treason, and his crown lost on the
  Boyne.

Erin, lament that luckless day, and veil thy widowed head,
Th' usurper waved his reeking sword above thy heroes dead.
The shamrock withers on thy hills! Thy locks with cypress
    twine !
Thy loyal heart was drowned in blood upon the field of Boyne !

SUNDAY BICYCLE RIDING.

——:o:——

One fine Sunday morning, for health or diversion,
Three bicycle riders would have an excursion ;
And 'twas publish'd abroad that each stalwart young stager
Would ride for his life, or a ruinous wager ;
Hurrahs from the Bowling Green rose as they started,
And buckled and strapped, the three gallants departed,

Up Cheapside they sped, and on Manningham Lane,
Like engines broke loose, or a runaway train ;
The church-goers stared, and each church-going bell,
Seem'd ringing " ding dong, they are riding to hell !"
And they saw an old woman a haystack pursue,
As on by Red Beck and by Shipley they flew.

But black thunder-gloom in the air 'gan to brood
Over arcades of trees as they enter Nab-wood ;
And onward they rode, though not quite so elated,
For demons their bicycles all animated ;
To brake or to stay as the darkness grew thicker,
Was useless—and on they flew wilder and quicker.

" The deuce ! we are going like mad !" cried Ned Wray,
" My bicycle's leaping and running away,
We are rolling down hill, and 'tis dark as a boot,
It is dangerous, lads—I wish I was a-foot !"
And the road still grew steeper, and blacker and higher,
The tree boles 'gan burning like columns of fire.

By this terrible light Neddy saw in his rear
His mates like two goblins on hippogriffs near ;
Undefined all around he saw horror's dread forms,
And the wood groan'd and roar'd like the ocean in storms—
To stop his curs'd bicycle, Nedly e saye l,
But he gave it new life by the efforts he made !

And still he heard pealing the parish church bell,
Bob major, " ding dong, they are riding to hell !"
And a gate arching high, like a church-porch they near'd,

And folding doors opening, and red-hot appear'd ;
Ned strove to resist, but on, on, they still sped,
" Lord save us !" he prayed, " 'Tis all over with Ned !"

With these words and a spring, and a terrific roar,
From his bicycle fiend he fell squelch on the floor ;
And amazed he awoke, his poor wife loudly screaming,
" Ned, Ned, what's the matter ?" Quoth he, " I've been
    dreaming !
My nose, knees, and elbows I've hurt—strike a light !
Thank goodness I'm safe—what a terrible fright !

'Tis the nightmare, mayhap, I have just been bestriding,
Or a warning 'gainst Sabbath-day bicycle riding ;
Or conscience has conjured up old superstition,
But I feel in quandarious thirsty condition !"
Said his wife, and she laugh'd, " but one word will explain
Both the cause and effect, and that word is—Champagne !"

THE CABBAGE AND ROSE.

Pater mihi sæpe dixit,
Studium quid inutile tentas.
Thus old daddy often spake,
Verses, lad, ne'er butter'd cake.—OVID.

A POET once, in leisure hour,
Had learnt the speech of plant and flower,
And listening in the sun, at ease,
The serenades of birds and bees,
He heard, in words of bitterness,
A cabbage thus a rose address : —

" Thou useless shrub, miscall'd a tree,
What in the world's economy
Art thou ? Where is thine use or good ?
Hunger rejects thy hips for food ;
I marvel gardeners can't see
The worthlessness of things like thee.
'Tis strange that maidens young and fair,
Should prank thee in their shining hair ;
But girls are weak, I own with grief,
They ought to wear a cabbage leaf.
Their mother's pass and note thee not
When culling kail for dinner pot.
Out of my sight—begone—depart !
Thy thorns discover what thou art."

"Patience," the noble rose replied,
" I am the garden's greatest pride,
Love's bright emblem banner-borne,
On the crown's of monarchs worn.
My odours o'er the billows come,
In otto from the land of Roum ;
My ancestors of Sharon yet
Adorn the page of Holy Writ.
Where'er a youth sees beauty, he
Delighted says, 'Tis just like me ;
So hogsmeat, hold thy railing tongue,
Feed, fatten, bloat upon thy dung.
Gross fool, I paint Aurora's brow,
Whilst food of swine and maggots thou.
We both are useful, but I find
Thou'rt for the paunch, I for the mind."

The poet muttered in his turn,
" A body still may live and learn."

THE EXILE.

——:o:——

THE angels of love, of the season of youth,
Hover dim over the moorland streams ;
And the wild waving branks, with fingory leaves,
Point now to a land of dreams :
The loved and the lost one's shadowy forms
On the footpath of flowers yet I see,
Though I've been an alien long from the cuckoo's primrose song,
And the dales of the north countrie.

On the hearth of my father the stranger sits,
And sorrow-laden years have sped,
Yet my spirit often walks where the throstle sings,
With the green leaves over his head ;
Still the dark woods wave in the summer's south wind,
And the thunder-scathed gnarled oak tree
Is standing yet and stern, by the lily-kissing burn,
In the dales of the north countrie.

Why flies not memory with scenes ever dear ?
Why dies not the heart when young ?
Or why cruel destiny drive from the haunts
Where our lives and our loves first sprung ?

Though the stockdove at eve should forget to coo,
And the sun to drink the dew of the lea,
My memory of pain and affection shall remain
For the dales of the north countrie.

The hind will return to the brake of her youth,
And the swallow through the spring-clouds fly,
And the hare before the hound, in the coppice doubles round,
On her fern-shelter'd form to die ;
And fain would I rest in the dust of my sires,
While the wind pipes my monody,
And the restless peewit cries through the heather-purpled skies
In the dales of the north countrie.

Blow on in thy beauty thou damask rose,
Which the spring brings again and again,
To the home where an infant I saw the moon
Weirdly stare through the window pane !
Dance on generations of youth after youth,
As the spheres dance, and I shall not be
Where an angel of delight gathered elderberries bright,
In the dales of the north countrie.

THE RIFLEMAN.

——o——

O splendid ! I never beheld such a sight,
   If I don't go again 'twill go hard ;
Yes, Granny, spectators to view the sham fight
   Were as countless as flowers on the sward.

The riflemen wheeled, kneeled and ran all about
   As if mixed in a real battle fray ;
They kept charging like crazy, and firing at nought,
   And among them I spied Harry Gray.

There were rope-dancers, harlequins, ladies in gold,
   Spangled dresses and buskins and paint ;
And one, who was he ? ever handsome and bold,
   Guess, Granny, I'm certain you can't.

And Granny, you know, I had on my pink dress,
   And I'm sure I look'd smarter than they ;
One thought so I know, would he only confess,
   And a rifleman too—Harry Gray.

Hissing wildfires and rockets with terrible hum,
  Mixed with flying fat pigs filled the air,
And the din of the cannon, the trumpet and drum!
  Darling Granny, I wish you'd been there.

Hundreds danced on the daises in joy and delight,
  Till the close of the beautiful day,
And I, with a rifleman, linked home at night,
  Guess with whom, Granny guess—Harry Gray.

~~~~~~~~~~~~~~~~~~~~~~~

GAFFER REUBEN.

——:o:——

HEAR what Gaffer Reuben said?
" God, through nature, bids us wed ;
Wedded state is (all can tell)
Angel's heaven, demon's hell."

" List," now cried the ancient man,
  ' Experience is wise ;
When in the lists of love I ran
  I gain'd the fairest prize.

" I vow'd to bless my captive won,
  My oath in heaven was writ,
But, ere the earth roll'd round the sun,
  I learnt the word ' submit.'

" When rose domestic tempests dread
  And rain began to pour,
Dismayed, I hid my troubled head,
  And let the wrath drive o'er.

" The pride of merit on my brow,
  Ne'er sat with high pretence,
I recognised in weal or woe,
  The hand of Providence.

" My child was smit with death at play,
  My strength I saw depart,
No real joy since that sad day,
  Has visited my heart.

" Still hand in hand my dame and I
  Have wandered many years,
And ne'er for others grudg'd a sigh,
  For other's sorrows - tears.

" A humble and a contrite heart,
  In toil and care I prov'd ;
With patience and a little smart,
  I found myself belov'd."

Then up and spoke his ancient dame,
  " Why, man, your wig's awry,
Do let me right it ! See, for shame,
  Your twisted silken tie !

" When our first parents lived alone,
  Ere sin and sorrow came,
In persons two they were but one ;
  And Adam* was their name.

" When we were married we were two,
  Our inner loves unknown ;
Till time inclined, like drops of dew,
  And mingled us in one."   ·   .

An Angel's wing was seen to flit
  Athwart her visage plain,
A cup of ale she brought, and lit
  Her Reuben's pipe again.

GAFFER   REUBEN'S   SAW.

" The King's daughter is all glorious within."—Ps. xlv. 13.

HEAR what Gaffer Reuben said,
  While smoking at his door:
" My sons, the early love of truth,
  Unlocks celestial lore.
Judge not of fruits before unknown
  From husk, shell, pod or skin,
Nor from a maiden's outward mien
  What spirit dwells within.

" They say that Siddim's fruits are fair,
  But filled with noisome dust ;
And vines with grapes of poison tempt
  The palate's strongest lust.
They say the crocodile can weep,
  The panther purr and play,
And that the serpent fascinates
  With dulcet sounds its prey.

* And God blessed them, and called their name Adam.—Gen. v. 2.

i

" And fascinating beauty's wiles
    May screen a fiend within,
And painted gates and flowery paths,
    May lead to sinks of sin ;
The gesture meek, the downcast eye,
    The sweet and saint-like smile,
The sigh of pity for distress
    External eyes beguile.

" This world is but the outward husk,
    This body but the shell,
Of others glorious or dark,
    Of heaven or of hell.
For once I saw an angel bright
    Beneath an Indian skin ;
And would not own a pair of eyes
    Whose ken is not within.

" In trusting man or woman's faith
    Be cautious and beware ;
For hell puts heaven's raiment on
    To lure and to ensnare"—
He ceased, and Gammer Madge began
    To croon a song and spin ;
And Gaffer Reuben dashed his pipe,
    Arose, and went within.

TO MY MOTHER.

——:o:——

MANY springs have doff'd their robes
    And donn'd them on again,
And yet I feel thy gentle hand
    My aching head sustain.

And still I see thy humid eyes
    Through dim and spectral years,
And hear thine anguish in the moan
    That sooth'd my boyhood's fears.

The iron in the hand of old
    Has branded deep my brow,
Yet in night's watches oft I ask,
    Dear mother, where art thou ?

Not in the tomb (for earthborn minds
    That dwelling dark and drear)—

E

Earth could not hold thy tenderness,
  I may not seek thee there.

Thy home is Eden's gardens green,
  Thy heart in heaven's employ ;
There lives thy love as once it liv'd,
  But know'st thou yet thy boy ?

Silent, mother ? Silent ? No !
  Thy songs to me divine
I hear. My spirit ever will
  Hold sweet rapport with thine.

And in thy golden morning land,
  Time cancell'd and unseen
Unveils thy hidden loveliness,
  Nor hides what I have been.

With pansies, pinks, and peonies,
  Their constant fairy train,
Sweet birds to Burtreebanks have come,
  Sung, and away again.

'Twas there thou led'st thy dreamy boy
  The tender lambs to see,
And now o'er Eden's Burtreebanks
  His spirit goes with thee.

A TRIP TO MORECAMBE BAY.

ANNA took her silken scrip,
  And cheerily went her way
Upon a pleasant summer trip
  To famous Morecambe Bay.

From rambling round 'mong wonders new
  She sat upon the strand,
And gazed upon the waters blue
  And distant Westmoreland.

What ails the pretty maiden now
  She trembles in the gale ?
The rose tint now o'erspreads her brow—
  And now 'tis snowy pale !

A voice—Was it a mermaid nigh
  Singing with conch in hand ?
Or was it spirit minstrelsy
  Borne o'er the shingly strand ?

Low accents, soft as roseate dew,
  So sweetly, gently, fell—
Whence? but no mortal ever knew,
  And Anna does not tell.

It was a voice. It was no dream,
  Her ear was not deceived,
Words murmur'd in ambrosial stream,
  Pure, holy—and believed!

Smiled sunny hill and seabank green,
  Purple the billows roll'd
And on her bonny hand was seen
  The fiery flash of gold.

'Twas there she lost her crimson snood,
  And since 'tis many a day;
And Anna never yet has rued
  Her trip to Morecambe Bay.

THE SHEKINAH.

"I heard as it were a trumpet talking with me, which said, "Come up
hither.'"—Rev. 14. 1.

From Hades dim abyss I cried, as spectres came and went,
I knew not what or whence they were, and marvell'd what they
   meant;
There were Ojiim and evening wolves and dancing Satyrs nigh,
And serpents breathing pestilence, but Mercy heard my cry;
And sudden as the storm-bolt lifts the veil of nightly skies
On adamantine columns borne, I saw a temple rise,
The structures of Persepolis, Diana, Libyan Jove,
All Grecian, all Mizraim's fanes in hallow'd mount or grove,
The Hebrew fabric and the towers rear'd by th' Assyrian queen
Compared were icons, built by spirits, earthly, gross and mean:
Of tempest pinion'd Cherubim each buckler seem'd a moon
Ablaze with beams from inner heaven's open-window'd noon,
And the trumpet-blast of Sinai continuous and loud
Proclaim'd the mystic tabernacle— Shekinah of God!
A golden throne with six bright steps of priceless gems appeared
And lions six on either hand tremendous guardians glared,
And closely veiled upon the throne a minstrel smote his lyre,
And men in myriads listened to his voice and golden wire—
'Twas Moses. Of chaotic gloom, Creation, of the birth
Of man, the Fall, the Flood, and the division of the earth,

Of Abraham, Isaac, Israel, Jehovah's works he sung,
Then down in disappearing his magic harp he flung.
I then beheld a regal form ascend and grasp the lyre,
His eyes were fierce as meteors, his words like tongues of fire,
To themes of blood and strife, and prayer and praise, his fingers
    flew
Across the harp, and David's bold and kingly voice I knew,
He faded like a phantom, and once more upon the throne
A monarch seized the harp, a hierarch of wisdom's own ;
In gold of Uphaz, gem-emboss'd, and blue and purple drest,
He glimmer'd like a seraph in the dayspring of the East ;
Surrounding him sang rosy choirs of Judah's daughters bright,
And flaming in habergeons, were ten thousand men of might ;
He caught the airs of angels as they hymned in glory's spheres,
And with truth's mystic " song of songs " he moved the world
    to tears ;
He raised his hand and smote the harp with fierce magician's
    sweep,
And tempest-borne at his command came genii of the deep,
Dark spirits at his footstool bent—his slaves—and by them he
Built Tadmor in the wilderness, Beth-horon on the sea.
He faded : and an ancient man, with beard as winter white
Ascended, rapt—a vision'd Seer—and lost in inward light—
Isaiah. Future times he sung and happier days to be,
When the sunlight should be sevenfold, and clouds and shadows
    flee,
When a child should lead the forest king, the changeful moon
    should cease,
And 'neath their vines and fig-trees men securely rest in peace,
The King of mystic Israel assume the diadem,
And His captive people, freed, again behold Jerusalem—
The PRINCE he sung, excelsior swell'd his harp's celestial tone,
And as he swept its radiant chord I gazed and he was gone—
And slowly in a starry robe I saw another rise,
Celestial halos zoned his head, and flames shot from his eyes ;
He took the harp and awful sounds came from each trembling
    chord,
For he sung of heaven's appearance and the chariot of the Lord :
Fear like a shadow fell among the silent listening throng
And deep amaze, as loud and wild and wondrous roll'd his song,
Ezekiel's voice I heard, I look'd to see the workings of his face,
But he was gone and weeping sore another fill'd his place.
His strains were lamentations and agonizing woe,
The sorrows of captivity, the proud insulting foe :
Like howling storms that through the midnight vault of winter
    sweep,

Like hollow roar of waters in the black and tumbling deep,
Like outer desolation's sound his dreary harp was heard,
Ono long-drawn groan his strain, and Jeremiah disappear'd—
And humbled—bending to the dust—I heard the LoGos say
" Up, son of man! Arise! Up hither come away "

A FATHER'S LAMENT.

"I shall go to him, but he shall not return to me." 2nd. Samuel, xxiii. 11

AGAIN, again, that sight of mourning!
    On my brain that maddening scene!
Stark, and cold, and still my darling!
    Dead! not dead? What can it mean

Fill the bowl—heaven's mercy slumbers,
    Endite my heart a funeral strain;
Sorrow is the nurse of numbers,
    Poesy the child of pain.

Close to life are others clinging,
    Sweetly past their moments flee;
But to me their wings are bringing,
    Nerveless—hopeless misery.

Happy he whose heart's affections
    Are not rudely torn away,
Full of pleasant recollections,
    Comes unnoted life's decay.

Happy with his offspring round him,
    In their youth his youth renews,
Blooming love that early found him,
    Blossoming again he views.

Time his locks with frost adorning,
    In his increase finds him blest,
And at last his children mourning,
    Bear him gently to his rest.

I—alone—bereft—forsaken,
    Have no child to smile or weep;
None my energies to waken,
    None to lull my cares to sleep.

Seasons going, seasons coming,
    In their rounds to me the same,
Flowers fading, flowers blooming,
    Grief's attention only claim,

Happy wild birds billing kindly,
  In the morning of the year,
Heavenly instincts serving blindly,
  Take your meed from me—a tear.

Earth grows cold, and sun spots gather,
  Grave worms round my senses creep ;
May Thy will be done my Father,
  Give, oh give my spirit sleep !

Wealth is but a maniac's bauble,
  Fame—a vain and empty dream,
Honour—heaviness, and trouble,
  Life—a fitful winter gleam.

Turn my soul to life's to-morrow,
  Heaven opens on my sight !
Lo ! another new aurora
  Rising on this mundane night.

Mercy ! memory still is burning
  On my brain that maddening scene,
Stark, and cold, and still my darling,
  Would that I had never been.

THE BACHELOR FROM LOVE.

——:o:——

How happy once the early morn,
When summer robed the scented thorn,
When nature blessed the golden ray
In greenwood hymns sung far away,—
  Listen from Eden, Genevieve !
I loved thee then, I love thee now
As tenderly as long ago ;
Long loved, long lost ! Those warm blue skies
Delight no more mine aged eyes,
  My heart went with thee, Genevieve.

Love yet deceives, for in my dreams
I roam beside my native streams,
Thou by my side ; nor am I old,
Nor is thy love-glance quench'd and cold,—
  Listen from Eden, Genevieve !
I speak again of coming joy,

A hopeful, careless, ardent boy,
And thy replies are soft and clear,
And dove-like as long since they were,
    And thou art faithful, Genevieve.

Ah, hopes! ah, pleasures! all gone by;
Ah, fruitless love and transient joy,
Ah, summer fair whose smiles betrayed,
Ah, loved, ah, lost, regretted maid,—
    Listen from Eden, Genevieve!
My pilgrimage will soon be o'er,
And then we meet to part no more;
O'er Eden's sunlit plains we'll stray,
To live, to love, be blest for aye
    In angel wedlock, Genevieve.

DOOM OF BACHELORS FROM CHOICE.

One night in brown study in private séance,
I stared at the fire till I sunk into trance.
In such weakness or strength, if the truth all would own,
In ghost-seeing trances I am not alone;
For I saw that on earth we all wander a-kimbo,
In mists I saw lifted from bachelors' limbo.

'Twas a region eerie, vast, sultry, unclouded,
With thousands of spinsters and bachelors crowded;
As I entered, a beldame cried, "Where are you going?"
"I'm curious," I answered, "to see what you're doing.
What are those poor old fellows the women are beating
With distaffs and broomsticks, while toiling and sweating?"

"Those are upper-class fogies, judged only as fit
To fill up with rubbish the bottomless pit;
Old maids load their wheelbarrows, heaping them high,
Which they lift, groan, and wheel, while their drivers stand by,
And threaten with many a bang and a grin
To shunt them, along with their wheelbarrows, in.

"Of the middle-class tortures, turn round and behold
Those butterflies shining with purple and gold;
They were pleasures on earth they were keenly pursuing,
Of beauty and innocence seeking the ruin;
Here they can't choose but follow and clutch the gay things,
And grasp horrid scorpions with venomous stings.

" Of the cowardly poor, little better their lot :
Each is changed to an ass an old vixen has got ;
There goes one ;—see, she rides him like fury along,
Ceaseless, restless, with fiery spindle for prong ;
Through dark howling forests, by Phlegethon's river,
Up and down—up and down—limbo for ever.

" But perhaps you're the donkey for whom I have tarried,"
The Hecate exclaimed ; " Did you ever get married ?"
" Yes, hag ! " I returned ; and perhaps I was plucky,
Or simple, or wise, but I find I was lucky :
When a shot from the grate of a coffin or purse
Burnt my nose, and I woke ;—and I might have done worse.

THE WITCH: A WINTER'S TALE.

——:o:——

In olden time when Robin Hood
Enjoy'd King Richard's grace,
And oft made Bradford in the wood
His sylvan trysting place,
When the bugle winded on the breeze
From outlaws night and day,
And squirrels leapt from old Kirklees,
Among the ancient forest trees
To Kirkstall's abbey grey ;
When Bradford's youths were stout and true,
Its maids as pure as summer dew,
And want and care were seldom seen
Among the ings and holms of green,
Beside an oak in th' haunted hirst
And well where wild-boars slaked their thirst
A beldam dwelt—but whence she sprung
Is left by ancient bards unsung.
Hate lurk'd among her wrinkles deep,
Her laughter caused the flesh to creep,
The sinful strains at night she'd sing
Dark shadows o'er the moon would bring,
Low echoes moaned the burden dread.
And the ket-crow sat above her head.

SONG.

Come cummers a crone is no cumber,
No wither'd old fardel of lumber ;

For Asmodeus, her lord, she oft feasts at her board,
While honest folk quietly slumber !

Mildews and marsh vapours steep her,
As a night-mare she rides on the sleeper,
Like a cat unto death she will suck a child's breath,
And glare, curse, and spit at the weeper.

Two imps suck her dugs like two leeches,
As with filch'd human fibres she stitches
A shift that she's made from a shroud half-decayed,
For a dance at the Sabbath of witches.

She withers the heart that is sighing,
As through the night fog she is flying
On a besom amain, arm'd with dwale and henbane,
To poison the lips of the dying.

On a gibbet she sits like a spectre
In darkness where none can detect her,
When the wind swings the corse and the raven croaks hoarse
With her talons she is a dissector.

She drinks to Asmodeus her henchman,
And shrieks as the ghosts of the slain can ;
Her liquor is brew'd from the rabid wolf's blood
And quaffed from a murderer's brain-pan.

   Her tasks at midnight she pursued,
   And henbane, dill, and nightshade brew'd,
   And her familiar brought her warm
   From Erebus, spell, philtre, charm—
   And old sworn friends fell out and wrangled,
   And matrons with their husbands jangled,
   And youths began dissimulation,
   And maids to dress above their station,
   The smith 'gan forging bolts and locks,
   And beadles raised the parish stocks,
   And lawyers came in flocks like kites,
   And tipstaff knaves came round o' nights,
   Fists oft were clench'd and eye teeth-bare,
   Neighbours rugged their neighbours' hair,
   Dogs howl'd all night as if in dread,
   The poultry clock'd and wind-eggs laid,
   The bull went mad and gored the rams,
   Cows cast their calves, and ewes their lambs,
   The skrike-owl whoop'd at witching hour,
   And the old dame's ale and milk turn'd sour,
   And many a dreadful sign and omen,
   Foreboded still more mischief coming,

Till all bedevilled raised a curse
On her of all their ills the source.
At length a mighty tempest roar'd
And hail and fire together pour'd,
Tall trees went crashing to the ground,
And herds were kill'd and flocks were drown'd.
The clouds and night were black as pitch,
When a horrid clamour from the witch
Was heard for miles—and scorch'd and torn
Old Madge lay grinning dead at morn !

TO BRO. BEN, OF MOORCOCK HALL.

——:o:——

DEAR BEN,—

I really dreamt, 'twould seem ;
   For rationally speaking,
When folk are sleeping they should dream,
   And not when they are waking.

Me thought we up Parnassus' height
   Our weary way were wending,
And poets on our left and right
   Were noisily ascending.

In fact, dear Ben, there seem'd a host,
   Elbowing everybody,
Swagg'd with religious mungo dust
   And sentimental shoddy.

The coarse and vulgar dialect
   Of some excited pity ;
To bear clown's jargon we expect
   Something at least that's witty.

"Come on, old chum !" I cried, " this noise
   Is past my patient bearing ;
We'll leave these scrannel poet boys
   To those who give them hearing,"

Soon on the mountain's head, "cloud-capp'd,"
   We saw a temple tower,
With gates fast closed, at which we rapp'd
   At least a full clock hour.

"Ben, take up stick or stone," said I,
  "My teeth begin to chatter,
'Tis horrid cold so near the sky;
  We'll make a rousing clatter."

We bang'd like mad, and open wide
  The portals flew like thunder,
And scenes appeared on every side
  That struck us dumb with wonder:

Apollo sate on cloudy throne,
  On starry "Lyra" strumming;
The tuneful "Nine" around him shone,
  Banjos and fiddles thrumming;

And mighty bards, all laurel crown'd,
  Were banqueting and singing;
Carousal through and all around
  The ancient fane was ringing.

"See, Ben," says I, "there Pegasus
  Good nectar drinks like water!
Let's in; There's luck at last for us,
  Our flanks will soon be fatter."

When "Back my master's! What's your will?"
  Was shouted just beside us—
And who d'ye think it was but Bill
  Wordsworth? Mercy guide us!

"What's that to you," I answered; "we
  Came hither on adventure;
Like you we've spun some rhymes, d'ye see,
  And like you we will enter."

"Is that your game," growled he. "Ho! Burns,
  Thy clogs and tough plough scraper!
This knave my post of porter spurns,
  Just gar the fellows caper."

Burns came, half drunk, from nectar can,
  Bold, beautiful and burly;
And down the hills we turned and ran,
  For faith his looks were surly.

I woke about the dawn of day,
  My heart with terror throbbing,
And on my bed I shivering lay,
  As naked as a robin.

WILLIE O'MEARY'S PIG.

——:o:——

Says Hetty, says hoo, " we're all sinners," says hoo,
" But my word is worth some women's bond,
Haworth folk are all conny and thrifty you know,
They certainly think their church steeple too low,
But they do not manure it to see if 'twill grow,
Nor rake for the moon in the pond.

Willie O'Mearys once bought a young pig,
It was one of Tom Grindlestone's breed.
And he left it to hunt for its grub, and to dig
In the gutters and sinks, till it grew up so big
That he thought he would give it a feed.

So a bag of small warty potatoes he bought,
And some pailfuls of thin stinking swill,
And a stone of rough bran mix'd with sawdust he got;
And a limb of horse-ket for a stomachic brought,
But never a handful of meal.

Then he kill'd it ; and talk went the country round,
From Ponden all down to Stock-brig,
That a back-load of thibles and ladles were found
In its belly ;—and juries of gossips were bound
That Willie had murdered his pig !

I remember the day as 'twere yesterday still ;
For I'd just got my bed of our Donty.
And Malley O'Shallocks had christen'd their Bill,
And the rain burst the bog on the top of Crowhill
That frightened our good parson Bronté.

And that very same night there were yellocks and screams,
So that Haworth all sweated in bed ;
For the rain they say hiss'd in the lightning's red streams,—
And hung with his pig upon one of his beams
In the morning was Willie found dead !

And whether or not ghosts come out for fresh air
I leave to the knowing and wise,
And whether you trust me or not I don't care,
But in ghosts I believe, and I freely declare
What hundreds have seen with their eyes.

For ever since then in the night thunder blast
Running fast may be seen Willie's ghost,

And his pig with a poke in its snout grunting past
At his heels, for the meal it was robb'd of a taste,
Till back to his grave Willie hurries at last,
And both in the darkness are lost.

THE DOG AND HARE.—A Fable.*

By Napoleon Buonaparte I.

Aide toi et Dieu t'aidera.

Young Pompey was a dog of price and note,
A liver-coloured spaniel fleet of foot,
One day when snifting round for game,
Lurk'd on her form he found a hare ;
" Surrender !" he cried, " I have you there.
Pompey the Great I am—well known for fame."
" And if I do surrender—what,"
Said puss, " will be my fate ?"
" Why, thou shalt die."
" And if I fly ?"
" Thy fate will be the same ;
I never lose my game."
" Well, then," said she, " since that's the case,
I'll try a race ;
' Tis better sure to try
'Gainst fate itself than sit and die."
And off she started o'er a log,
The sportsman saw her leap and run,
And levelling his gun,
He fired, and missed the hare and hit the dog.
That God helps those who help themselves, I say,
And would the great Lafontaine have said nay ?

* The above fable was written by Napoleon Buonaparte when a
student at the Military School at Brienne, in the sixteenth year of his
age, and translated from ' La Minerve,' a French Canadian newspaper,
dated 1830, by the Author.

A SUMMER LYRIC.

——:o:——

Rosalie ! O rosy hours,
Love-light's sheen on virgin flowers,
Sweets with sun-lov'd heavenly dyes,

Butterflies and dappled skies,
Honeydew on windy broom,
Pansy pink and clover bloom,
Incantation, harmony,
Beauty's spell and sorcery,
Orange wreath or cypress tree,
Love's first trance and—Rosalie !

Rosalie ! charm, grammarye,
Hesper's tear and Zephyr's sigh,
Lark ambitious, swallow fleet,
Throstle loud and linnet sweet,
Shadow floating o'er the corn,
Whispering leaf and beetle's horn
Fairy ring and haunted dell,
Kiss, embrace, and fond farewell,
Orange wreath or cypress tree—
Life's eclipse or Rosalie !

Rosalie ! from vocal grove
Mystic speech of magic love,
Thunder-burst from brow of Chevin,
Rifting, roaring, blinding levin,
Cloud-ship rigg'd with crimson sails,
Rain-arch bridging sparkling dales,
Hymn Eolian nightly sung,
Spirit's vigil, passion's tongue,
Orange wreath or cypress tree—
Courting gentle Rosalie !

Courting, wooing Rosalie,
Saffron hill and dreamy bee,
Thymy bank and heather bell,
Ladysmock and asphodel,
Meadowsweet and trysted bower,
Shepherd'sclock and witching hour,
Footpath lonely, shadow brown,
Dian chastely smiling down,
Orange wreath *no* cypress tree—
Wooing, WINNING Rosalie !

A HYMN.

Bear witness earth and heaven above
That love is God and God is love.—1 JOHN, iv, 7.

EVOLVE the fiery letter'd writ,
The Logos of the starry quires,

The lyric of the Infinite,
The gospel of Seraphic fires.
The temple glistens—in my heart ;
Sky music swells from Asaph's band
Invoke the royal Hebrew's art,
The Magus of the morning land.

There is a bright and golden strand,
Where underneath revolves the moon,
Where Glory waves his jewell'd wand
And angels sing in Eden's noon.
There sound the harps of myriads gone,
There youth and beauty brightly blend,
Love claims his own beloved one,
And sacred friendships know no end.

The sun sleeps in his rosy sheen,
On amaranthine mountains there,
No foot-print seen of death has been
To blight a joy or raise a tear ;
Celestial manna falls like dew,
Hope's sinking star they ne'er behold :
There living fountain's waters blue
Symphonious charm the age of gold.

Delirious bliss ; heights too sublime,
Imperial Love ascends His throne,
His speech through all that glorious clime,
Beatitude's hosannah's own,
Dash down the mundane harp—its voice
Is harsh as winter's midnight storm,
Ye heaven of heavens and earth rejoice,
God magnifies his humble worm.

THE SKYLARK.

—— :o: ——

THE son of Aurora was up in the sky,
The boundless, mysterious, terrible sky,
The bard in his mood saw the race on the rye,
Shadows pursuing the lights on the rye.
"Tell me," said he, "happy bird of the morn,
"What is the meed of thy musical treat,
Wert thou not better in blossom and corn,
Gathering dew-worms below with thy mate?"

" Read me, O bard, on my minaret dim,
  Read Nature's volume of wisdom sublime,
Mine is the mystical language of Him,
  The still and small voice from the altar of Him.
Birds of the cloudland and birds of the bower,
  Sounds from the shades of the wilderness grim,
Lamb tempests booming, and hailstorms that pour,
  Are but the wonderful organs of Him.

" See'st thou His arm, with His brand and His bow;
  Can'st thou divine the deep myths of the pole?
Read'st thou His name, as the characters glow,
  Inwove in His glorious aureole?
Love in my bosom and joy on my wing —
  Breasting the winds as they merrily go;
Listen my pipe, as the angel of Spring,
  Raining a torrent of silver below.

" Up with the strain to mid-heaven again,
  Merrily O, so merrily, O;
Wisdom is plain in the wind and the rain,
  Innocence ever sang cheerily, O.
Know'st thou the gamut of planet and star?
  Fill'd with their melodies, ether I swim.
Syrian sages, with reverent ear,
  Wrote on their hearts the dark sayings of Him."

Rapt was the minstrel in visions of Love—
  Love but revealed to the children of love—
Windows of heaven were opened above,
  Deluging glories from oceans above.
Sing, happy lark, while the elements roar,
  Steps of the ladder of Jacob we climb,
Like thee and Seraphim, singing we soar,
  When we become but the organs of Him.

MERRITED TRUE LOVE.

——o——

'TWAS not because my Ann Carlyle,
  Had locks as dark as night,
Or through her modest dimpling smile
  Her eyes flash'd heaven's light.
'Twas not because her neck was white

Its sun-kiss'd vestal snow,
Nor that her tiny feet were light,
I woo'd and lov'd her so.

'Twas not because retiring shame,
With trustful glances strove,
And rosy blushes went and came,
Whene'er I whispered love;
Nor that because her gentle breast
Was free from fraud and guile,—
Or virtue pure her soul had blest,
I wedded Ann Carlyle.

'Twas not that voice like music low,
From lips that knew no sin,
As birds sang from the chesnut bough,
And summer eves shut in;
It was not these made mine surpass,
Affection's common bound
But for her sleepless goodness 'twas,
That planted Eden round.

THE RAPARREE.

Sae rantingly, sae wantonly,
Sae dauntingly, gaed he,
He played a spring, and danced around,
Beneath the gallows tree.—OLD SONG.

His mother danced whin she was big
Wid Shan from night to morn,
And Shan kick'd up a Carrick jig
The minute he was born.
When but a gossoon in the dark
He danced wid Moyl's banshee,
And soon became St. Nichol's clark,—
A roaring rapparree.

He bang'd the durty Sassenach
Wid capers great and shmall;
Wid twinty divils on his track,
He danced troo Donegal.
He swore he'd tache the Saxon Queen
A riggadoon to dance;
Whack big John Bull, the old spalpeen,
And kiss the dames of France.
He danced wid Biddy Flannagan,

F

And blue-eyed Kate Magee ;
And still they sigh in Monaghan
For Shan the rapparee.

He danced, that you would think 'twas jist
Like moonlight on the say,
Or like a shallop troó the mist
Up stormy Dublin Bay.
He danced old Erin oft across,
Wid fairies on the spree,
And dwelt in storms on moor and moss,—
Red Shan, the rapparree.

At whiskey keg, or pratee pot,
His likes you never saw ;
He was an Oirish pathriot,
And hated lord and law,
At last he danced a fearful spring,
And thousands came to see,
On nothing dance his farewell fling,
Bold Shan the rapparree.

Och, wishastrue ! come to his wake !
Och, hone ! bring shwipes galore ;
Lashings and lavings for his sake
Shall flood the shibbeen floor.
Shtroik up your poipes, ye durty baste,
The crather hand to me,
I'll give the purty corpse a taste,
The darlint rapparree.

PART OF THE SIXTH CHAPTER OF ST. MAT. VERSIFIED.

——:o:——

BEFORE ye ask—your Father's eyes,
Your needs with pity see ;
And in this pure and humble guise,
In spirit poor pray ye.
Our father in the heavens thy throne,
All hallow'd be thy name ;
Thy kingdom come Thy will be done,
In heaven and earth the same.

Still may we from thy bounty free,
Our daily bread receive ;

Forgive our many debts as we
Our debtors to forgive.
Lead not into temptatious thrall—
Cause evils far to flee,—
And kingdom power and glory all,
Thine evermore shall be.

A TRIBUTE TO THE MEMORY OF A FRIEND.

AGAIN, yawning grave, thou hast gulph'd up another,
Again, cruel death, thou hast flesh'd thy dread dart,
For the banqueting worm thou hast serv'd up a brother,
To gambol and feast in his excellent heart!

But we lift not the shroud the loath'd sight to uncover,
The wrecks of humanity sweetly shall rest;
But we ask thee, fell death, why thy wings seem to hover
O'er all, to make choice of the kindest and best.?

But thou hast thy mission, thy mandate from heaven,
'Tis mercy directs thee what bosom to hit;
And tho', as with thunder, scath'd, shatter'd, and riven,
Our hearts thou hast spared, we weep and submit.

'Tis finish'd his cruise at the fountain is broken,
Peace lulls his soft slumbers, and sits by his head,
The vengeance of grief and of sorrow is wroken,
The traveller is weary, and gone to his bed.

By fortune exalted aloft to mens's vision,
Then headlong to poverty suddenly cast;
By the same blind caprice, as the mark of derision,
Uprooted, he fell like an oak in the blast.

Blow on, wintry winds, for he marks not your yelling;
Drive, hail cloud, he recks not, he heeds not, thy roar;
Look coldly, thou sun, on his damp, narrow dwelling,
For warmth from thy beams shall revive him no more.

Come forth, lovely spring, in thy chaplets of flowers,
Thy wonted wild music, as erst never cease,
But careworn and heartless, he sought in thy bowers,
And found not, what death has restor'd to him,—peace.

Why chisel in marble his name and his story?
Why plant the dark cypress to shadow his urn?

His name is inscribed, in large letters of glory,
  On hearts, that no cypress needs beckon to mourn.

Dear friend ! thy tomb sounding lonely and hollow,
  Reminds us how shallow the draught of man's breath ;
We flourish awhile, then we fade and we follow
  Thy steps to the dim, silent chambers of death !

THE BANNER BLUE.

——:o:——

As floats a cloud on eddying gusts when tempests dire arise,
And vengeful winter raves and roars, the flag of England flies,
It floats as clouds of promise float that shade the thirsty plain;
When husbandmen prognosticate the summers' coming rain,
And e'er since when at Crecy and at Poictiers it flew .
Has Britain rested confident beneath the banner blue.

Our banner to our foreign foe is like the dread simoom,
Borne by Ballona burning blue o'er fields of blood and foam ;
Death madly rides along its path, and horrid is his frown,
As britons like strong reapers mow their iron legions down;
Imperial heads before it bow, and nations cringe and sue,
When freedom's dreadful whirlwinds rise and bear the banner
    blue.

Through wildest storms that ever roll'd the billows of the deep.
Our British navies ride along in grand victorious sweep ;
When murderous vollies boom, and thunder belching death and
    fear,
And hoary waves and blackened skies, a blazing girdle wear.
When red-hot balls like levin bolts to hate and vengeance true,
Shake earth and sky—its eagle flight still keeps our banner blue.

The bearing of the briton bold, his dignity and might,
The vastness of his treasury—his intellectual light ;
His honour and his bravery that set his island free,
A beacon-star for other lands, far shining o'er the sea ;
His art and science, peace and law, and his religion grew,
Encouraged and protected by the glorious banner blue.

A HYMN.

' Bless the Lord. O my soul, and forget not all His benefits. Ps. 103. 2.

    In earthly joys I'll ne'er forget,
      The mighty mind that taught ;

And gave me when in weakness left,
  The mystic strength I sought.

When in the midst of mirthfulness,
  And songs and jests go round ;
I'll think of Him who freedom gave,
  And loos'd my spirit bound.

When shines the sun of lovely June,
  From burning Leo's sphere ;
And gossamers float on the wind,
  And sounds of summer cheer.

When down the lawn the lev'rets rove,
  And round me hums the bee ;
And never tired of carolling,
  The throstle sits the tree.

When hare-bells drink the early dew,
  And merry stars appear ;
In scenes I lov'd in infancy,
  And unto manhood dear.

I'll think of Him who from mine eyes,
  The veil of error tore ;
And pointed to where summer reigns,
  And winter is no more.

ORIGIN OF THE CORN BILL.

(Written before the Repeal of the Corn Laws.)

As Lucifer sat in his council below
O'er debate to enforce his decision,
His muster roll conning, and marking it grow,
With fire-traced names for perdition :

Scrutinising dark deeds with accustomed care,
And judicial gravity over,
And thinking some sin from the world's upper air,
Of a novel design to discover.

None striking his eye but those hackney'd and worn,
Till their horrors seem'd scarce at all horrid,
" The features of death," he exclaimed with scorn,
" In England will soon be thought florid !"

Then harshly he call'd from his burning divan,
  Dark, moody, and fierce as a Gorgon ;

" Hark ye, Mammon, thou cleverest fiend of thy clan,
Thou'lt soon be my laziest organ ?

" Old England's hierarchy forms no new scheme
Of plausible human blood suction ;
Her mad Aristocracy dream the old dream,
Of honour and warlike destruction !

" Come ! hast thou no scourge to her governments' taste—
New treachery, fraud, or coercion ?
If thou hast, bring it out with all possible haste,
We want it for further diversion !''

" Why, I've one,'' growled Mammon (and bowed) ''that I made,
But I fear'd it would scarcely be civil,
To bring't into court, for 'tis really *too* bad,
Even to offer to *you*, my lord Devil !

" It is a quintessence of every crime ;
It will ruin the mightiest nation ;
A foul pestilential abortion of time ;
'Tis a DEARTH-BILL FOR GRISLY STARVATION !''

Each fiend started back, and all Hell gave a shout,
Till earth heard the loud acclamation ;
And all the grim senate with Mammon rushed out
To see it in quick operation.

SONG.

——:o:——

Young Oswald rode down yonder glen,
   Sing dewy meads are bonny :
Young Araminta met his ken,
   When banks of Aire were sunny.

Do angels sometimes visit here,
   Sing Throstles call so cheerly ;
Be mine, my love, my only dear,
   For linnets wake so early.

They lov'd they kiss'd while leaves were green
   Sing Flora smiles but curtly ;
And Oswald came, and went unseen,
   The cuckoo sings but shortly.

Aye, clasp thy baby to thy breast,
  Sing Joy we taste but barely;
Forever lost thy virgin rest,
  We pay for pleasure dearly.

OLD DONALD'S LAMENT.

——:o:——

No more bonny Scotland, though happy and braw,
  Though thy mavis and lavrock sing still through the lea,
No more the lov'd songs of the strath and the shaw,
  Or the cloud-kilted mountains are charming to me.
The wild spreading hawthorn in sweet summer bloom,
  The breeze of the gloaming that plays with the broom,
Or the burn rushing past like a war-horse in foam,
  Cheer not an old bosom that's weary and wae.

No more the snell storm that sets dark in the lift,
  When the shelterless woods of old Scotia are brown,
When the birdies cheep sorely to see the white drift,
  And the blue-bells and gowans are faded and gone.
No more the long tale of the clansmen's dark feud
  The wild song of battle that rouses the blood,
Or the loud ringing laugh and the kiss oft renewed,
  That still charm the long winter can banish my wae.

Long, long, has my Annie laid mouldering and cold,
  The friend of my bosom has long ago gone,
The kye that I tended have long left the fold,
  And the cot which I builded is roofless and lone,
My frame is all crippled, my hair is like snow,
  The pastime of nature distresses me now;
My measure is full and I long to lie low,
  And cast off the old shell, for I'm weary and wae.

The glamour of time has changed mountain and brae;
  Their loves and their pleasures, their music and bloom,
Seem ghosts of the past moaning coldly—away
  "Old Donald why linger so long from the tomb?"
I come to your halls of the peaceful and blest,
  To mix with the spirits of those I lov'd best,
Like the last lingering swallow forsook by the rest,
  That takes the dark ocean, all lonely and wae,

NATURAL AND SPIRITUAL SPRING.

———:0:———

'Tis a happy time for wandering,
　　When youth is in its glee,
When virgin spring is squandering
　　Her jewels o'er the lea.
When by the stream meandering,
　　Birds sing from tree to tree,
And winters tempests thundering,
　　Give way to Zephyrs free.

When the bonny moon unclosing
　　Her silver chamber door,
Walks o'er the mountains dozing
　　Upon her starry floor.
Whilst love is soft reposing,
　　In yet unblighted flower,
Or on the dew carousing,
　　In mornings golden hour.

Blest spring of souls awaking,
　　When wintry time is past ;
When light and life are breaking
　　Their mortal bonds at last.
When cheerfully forsaking
　　Earths cold and barren waste,
With thy day of farewell taking,
　　Haste on thy pinions haste.

Heavens mountains in the morning,
　　In purple light appear,
Life's trees to flower returning,
　　Their varied mantles wear.
Where the heart new songs is learning,
　　To bless the sabbath year,
My soul is inly burning,
　　For Love's green dwellings there.

A SIGH FOR LORD BROUGHAM.

———:0:———

EARTH to earth and dust to dust !
　　In death's cold chambers room, more room !

Crowds into their portals thrust:
  Room for millions yet to come.

Moulder, monument and bust;
  Moulder fast: more room, more room!
'Scutcheons over 'scutcheons thrust,
  Countless 'scutcheons yet to come.

Soul and body, tomb and name,
  Memorials of the past, make way:
Dim and dimmer wanes your fame,
  Behind the famous of to-day

Thinner grow your misty forms,
  Ye mighty and renowned of yore;
Faster feed yo hungry worms,
  The grave is howling "More, give more!"

Lore, ambition, love, and crime,
  Make way, make way for others nigh;
Ripples on the flood of time,
  Gilded bubbles, hurry by.

Flow on, ye cataracts of tears,
  Through generations onward flow;
Increasing with revolving years.
  Flow sadly to the gulf of woe.

Go, Brougham, go, in Lethe's stream,
  Among the great and good forgot;
Fade like a bright but transient beam:
  Even thine must be the common lot.

Moulder, monument and bust;
  Moulder fast: more room, more room!
'Scutcheon over 'scutcheon thrust,
  Countless 'scutcheons yet to come.

TO MY NEW BORN CHILD.

———:0:———

From the womb all fresh and bright,
  Stranger welcome to the light;
Object of a father's cares.
  Subject of a mother's prayers;
Unto life's unhappy vale,
  Pure immortal spirit hail.

In thine infant features shine,
  Angel's lineaments divine;
In thy sweetly dawning smile,
  Lurks no trace of fraud or guile,
Thy young heart unstain'd with sin;
  Beats to heaven's strains within.

As in rosy vernal hour,
  Opes to light the tender flower;
From thy maker fresh art thou.
  Beautious as the mornings brow,
Emanation from above,
  Fair as new created love.

Softly on thy mother's knee,
  Sleep—affection cradles thee;
Sleep, whilst angels in thy rest
  Charm with music of the blest,
Time in tears thine eyes may steep;
  Sorrow soon forbid to sleep.

Hygeian airs thy steps attend,
  Truth be thine instructing friend;
Heaven opening on thine age,
  Light thee from this mortal stage;
Smiles and blessings welcome thee,
  Child of immortality.

TO MARY.

——:o:——

In short liv'd beauty, Mary,
  Earth's flowers expose their dyes,
But there's a region, Mary,
  Where flowers of life arise.
In the sunbeams of th' Eternal,
  They ope their radiant eyes,
For delights for ever vernal
  Are the blossoms of the skies.

There are comely features, Mary,
  Where evil fills the breast,
And forms of beauty, Mary,
  Where serpents make their nest.

But inward beauty's traces,
　　Are wisdom's true love test
And affection's sunny graces
　　Form the faces of the blest.

In outward beauty, Mary,
　　Thou canst with any shine,
Let inward beauty, Mary,
　　In constant bloom be thine.
For here the sickly blossom
　　May shortly fade and pine ;
But the blossom of the bosom
　　Shall bloom in climes divine.

Though thou'rt neglected, Mary,
　　Teach not thine eyes to rove ;
Earth's love is fickle, Mary,
　　Unchanging heaven is love ;
Affections here unspoken
　　Are sweetly interwove ;
There is heal'd the heart that's broken—
　　The sad are cheer'd above.

LOVE.

——:o:——

Love enters the heart when 'tis tender and young,
And its rich Eden blossoms unfold ;
He looks through the eyes and he sits on the tongue,
And he whispers of joys never said, never sung,
In Saturnian ages of gold.

He seeks the rude cot of the humble and poor,
And the riches of Ormus he brings ;
He enters the palace, and sadness no more
Dims the sheen of its pomp, For he lives at the core
Of the hopes and the pleasures of kings.

He breathes on the earth, and 'tis covered with flowers—
Silver fountains in melody spring ;
He looks from the east, and the rosy lip'd hours,
Come dancing to waken the birds in the bowers,
'Mong the green leaves to warble and wing.

He curbs the black surge when at midnight 'tis rolled
To the wan moon in tempest sublime,
And the isles of the ocean their glories unfold,

Like emeralds, cinctured with azure and gold,
As the first emanations of time.

Like a regal magician he waves his weird wand,
And smooths hoary winter's rough brow;
And the storm enthroned thunders that howl o'er the land
Are hush'd. With a touch of his beautiful hand—
Burn with crimson the mountains of snow.

He strikes the bright chords of the spheres, and they ring
Through the deep diapason divine;
And the garlanded angels the brightest stars bring,
From creation's blue confines, to crown him a king,
In the mid empyrean to shine.

THE SAILOR.

——:o:——

Summer roses blithly blow,
    Summer suns are beaming, Love;
Happy nature singing now
    Seems of Eden dreaming, Love:
Beauty, health, and wealth are mine,
    Servants round me handy, Love;
Jewels, silks, and velvets fine—
    But, oh! I have not Sandy, Love!

He left me with a rising tear,
    He bade me still be cheery, Love;
But till his flag again appears,
    I'll weep and ne'er be weary, Love.
In jacket blue and Albert chain.
    He is a tarry dandy, Love;
He cruises on the Spanish main,
    My jovial sailor Sandy, Love

He merrily dances on his craft,
    Boreas for his piper, Love:
O'er the snoring seas abaft
    Cheerily shouts my skipper, Love;
I've winks, and smiles, and blushes red
    From rollicking lads and randy, Love;
But I will only, only wed
    With bold and burly Sandy, Love.

When down the lawn young feet are light,
    And barely ding the daisy, Love,
When lips are luscious, eyes are bright,
    And mirth runs wild and mazy, Love,
When many a stolen kiss is felt
    Like candy dipped in brandy, Love,
My weary heart begins to melt
    To tears for absent Sandy, Love!

THE COQUETTE.

——:o:——

SUMMER was young and barley green,
    Blossoms had snowed the way;
When Emily sighed in leafy screen,—
    " I am twenty-nine to-day!

" Unmarried, unhappy, and all alone,
    By folly and pride betrayed,
My jilted lovers have one by one
    Resigned me to die a maid!

" O woe betide my stars and me,
    To linger, by love unblest;
An apple to wither upon the tree,
    A flower on no one's breast!"

Her eyes were wet; a swain she met:
    Good heaven, but she was fain!
When he sang to the rueful sad coquette
    An old song over again.

" Heigh ho! marry me, love!
    Roses soon decay;
Mine is the heart of the gentle dove
    That lends the loves of May.

" Summer dews are falling chill,
    Nightingales I hear;
But thy sweet accents ever will
    To me be doubly dear.

" No squire am I of gentle grade,—
    My hand and heart are free,—
I am but a simple snip by trade,
    And humble my degree.

" Sing thimbledum, needledum, marry me, dear ;
    Pity to say me nay ;
Cabbage and goose is dainty cheer,
    Remnant fents are gay."

Then, all unheard, like mateless bird,
    She sang in an undertone,—
" Humph ! ha ! a tailor ! good Lord !
    Well ! any, good Lord, and soon !"

A SERENADE.

——:o:——

FAIRIES wear garments the star-glances weave ;
    Aileen na Eireen, oh Aileen aroon !
Come like the dew to the bosom of eve ;
    Aileen na Eireen, oh Aileen aroon.
Love leads the brave o'er the dark, boiling main ;
Love will return to his nest back again.
Aileen na Eireen, oh Aileen aroon !
Aileen na Eireen, oh Aileen aroon !

    Myrtle groves whisper " Why lingers my dear ?"
    Aileen na Eireen, oh Aileen aroon !
None but the angels of beauty are near,
    Aileen na Eireen, oh Aileen aroon !
Think of thy tryst, for no more we may meet :
Fair blows the wind and impatient the fleet.
Aileen na Eireen, oh Aileen aroon !
Aileen na Eireen, oh Aileen aroon !

    Laurels are gather'd in tempest and flame ;
    Aileen na Eireen, oh Aileen aroon !
Danger is guard over glory and fame ;
    Aileen na Eireen, oh Aileen aroon !
Maid of Avoca, I languish alone,
Naiads are singing and bathing the moon ;
Aileen na Eireen, oh Aileen aroon !
Aileen na Eireen, oh Aileen aroon !

    Mariners dare the wild breakers ahead ;
    Aileen na Eireen, oh Aileen aroon,
Love is their shield when the battle is red ;
    Aileen na Eireen, oh Aileen aroon ;

Speak but once only and cheer my fond heart,
Smile but once only before I depart ;
Aileen na Eireen, oh Aileen aroon !
Aileen na Eireen, oh Aileen aroon !

THE GENIUS OF MAN.

'TWAS when green summer was gone,
  And rustling leaves were sere,
And stacks were thatched and harvest done,
  And plenty crowned the year.

Not a bird gave a friendly trill,
  Save robin upon the byre,
For far away o'er copse and hill
  Had flitted the plumy quire.

When by the wayside, with beard,
  Like mist on November's sky,
Sitting I found a stranger wierd,
  Who beckoned as I passed by.

"Old man, is it charity
  Thy sore distress would crave ?
In sooth I've litt e to give to thee,
  E'en should I give all I have.

With a grin of derision he said,
  "On a bright and golden day,
God's legate of charity, earthward I sped,
  But coveted wealth and sway.

I was one of the first to rebel,
  With Satan I led the van,
And down with the infidel crew I fell,
  And the Iron age began.

With murderous engines armed
  I mounted Bellona's car,
And earth and hell together alarmed
  With the flame cyclones of war.

My burning chariots run
  Horseless in dread career,
My messengers far outstrip the sun
  To the gaol of the rolling year.

I measure the morning star
  The moonland's regions trace,
I ride the comet, the herald of war,
  To his stall in th' abyss of space.

Creations passed away,
  I call from their tombs of earth,
And the uncouth forms of Time's first day
  In hideous life come forth.

I open the gates of light,
  Unbar the doors of gloom,
Bring forth the unborn horrors of night,
  Or births from the morning's womb.

With me both the Church and State
  To the demon of 'selfhood' bow,
My ministers mete out human fate—
  Omnipotent here below.

My favours I heap on the few,
  And the many are quite forgot,
Though my mission unknown to the infidel crew
  Was to better humanity's lot."

"Enough, dread figure, enough,
  But wherefore so far away
From heavenly duty—pity proof,
  Still unrepentant, say?"

Like a demon he frowned and passed
  Away from the cold grey stone;
And poverty called in the biting blast
  On merciless genius gone.

WOMAN.

TO THE FRIENDS OF FEMININE ENFRANCHISEMENT.

THAT the male represents understanding alone,
  May be seen from his form, feature, bearing, and tone,
And the female its constant affection;
  In heaven, earth, hell, both the sexes are one,
And from Scripture and Nature the fiat has gone—
  "Beware how you break the connection."

Woman, man's duplicate, outer man, mate,

Is his own alter ipse, soul's speculum, fate,
He her inmost ; as she is his outer ;
    He plays on her every affection at will,
    And woe unto tact, talent, genius, or skill
        That would live, thrive, or flourish, without her.

She's a wanton and frow with the Latter-Day Saints ;
    With the Ranter she wrestles, and shrieks till she faints,
When the ears of the pious, he's dinning ;
    With the Friends she is mute, in a leaden hued hat,
Unsex'd as a nun ; with the Church of the State
    She'll crow " as it was in the beginning."

She's the soldier's dear trull and the sailor's pet callet,
    A queen to a king, and a cadger's safe wallet,
Will rake with the rakes deepest folly ;
    She mates with philosopher, statesman, and e'en
When matched for her sins with a poet, I've seen
    Her jauntily wear the green holly.

She weds at a venture and misery dares,
    Unravels the most complicated affairs ;
And (this secret I don't wish to go forth
    For heaven forefend I should slander or vex),
'Tis said, aye, and sung, that the scum of the sex
    For base kelter would marry—and so forth.

More than brother to brother a sister is dear ;
    To her more than mother a father is near,
Though both were base, brutal, and callous ;
    A mother will cling with death-grasp to her son,
And though crimson'd with crime, to her arms he can run,
    When a fugitive, chased by the gallows.

Savage or civil, as man's bad or good,
    Personified passion of every mood,
She's man's wife, marrow, leman, and doxy ;
    His wealth, freedom, labours, and pleasures are hers,
Her lot is the first of his tenderest cares,
    And her vote will be always his proxy.

DUNRAVEN.

——:o:——

Even reign in my soul cried the gallant Dunraven ,
    Thou bright emanation of beauty and love ;
G

Though princesses smile bright as morn on Lochleven,
  No treacherous pulse in my bosom would move.

My heart's own young lord sigh'd the maid with emotion,
  We know not our hearts, and an earl's least of all;
I will wait one long year while you cross the vast ocean,
  Then pledge thee my troth in my ancestral hall,

At eve his last kiss on her lips he left glowing,
  The sun rising saw his white sail on the sea,
And soon the green shores of the Arno deep flowing,
  He trod with the step of the noble and free.

The rose bowers of Florence blushed bright at his coming,
  And princesses smiled as they saw him advance,
Proud was the dame that the Lord of Dunraven
  Selected to tread the light maze of the dance.

Then little reck'd he of his young bosom warming,
  As he strove the coy smiles of a stranger to win,
Little thought he of the danger so charming
  To his honour, his faith, and the maid of Lochlin.

"Dunraven," she sighed, as they stood by a fountain,
  " My troth to another is plighted and given,
My home is afar by the flood and the mountain,
  My vows are enrolled in the archives of heaven.

" Is there not one in thy Caledon loves thee,
  Not one distant maid thy heart throbs for alone,
Not one sacred pledge that a love-traitor proves thee?"
  " By heaven!" falsely answered Dunraven, " Not one."

Her veil laid aside—in the fountain's bright waters,
  She washed off the stain that had darkened her skin,
And before him she stood one of Caledon's daughters
  Outraged and betray'd the sweet maid of Lochlin.

She fled, and he wandered through foreign lands many,
  Again for his own the dear lost one to win,
And Dunraven grew grey, but he never found any
  To love like his dear mountain maid of Lochlin.

DISPUTE OF THE MUSICAL INSTRUMENTS.

——:o:——

One night as I pass'd by light of the gas,
  Near a musical instruments shop;

I heard a loud noise and to learn what there was,
   That occasioned it made a full stop.

With what wonder I stared, when from every nook
   Angry voices distinctly I heard ;
For as I'm alive every instrument spoke,
   And I'll strive to repeat every word.

Said Organ my lineage is old you all know,
   And the worship of God is my pride ;
I could drown all your voices when loudly I blow,
   That I'm chief never can be denied.

Heard ye that growl'd a deep hollow double Bassoon,
   Drown music aye, so may an ass ;
But I'll make it appear before everyone,
   The foundation of music is bass.

If you talk about chieftainship I must step forth,
   Squeak'd Fife then I think you'll be dumb,
I have led forth the Briton to conquer the earth
   With my rub-a-dub friend Kettle-drum.

What ! rung an upright Piano's rich tone,
   Greatest right to be chief I can show ;
With the nobles I dwell in the gilded saloon,
   And the queen's my admirer you know.

Then several shouted at once in a rage,
   With a loud gallimaufry din ;
And I heard an Hibernian bag-pipe engage,
   In a lilt and 'twas " Brian O'Linn.

Silence again in the shop was restor'd
   And a Harp in sweet accents began,
All poets have called me the instruments lord,
   Preferr'd both by angel and man.

In heaven—beg pardon—must speak Mr. Harp,
   Squeak'd a Fiddle. No poets believe ;
They can lie like the fiend—but we know the B sharp,
   We're too cute for their tales to deceive.

By all who've had any pretensions to taste,
   In my presence it oft has been said ;
That for scope I'm the chief so your breath do not waste,
   For the dance in all nations I've sped.

You the chief ! began Trumpet to lustily blow,
   I've a good mind your cat-guts to break ;
You're a silly ventriloquist all of us know,
   For it is from your belly you speak.

No violence! twenty call'd out in a breath,
    And directly I heard such a smash ;
I thought there are certainly bruises or death,
    For I heard the poor Fiddle cry crash.

But a crack of loud laughter within met my ear,
    Which I held as if nailed to the door ;
For the fool of a Fiddle in bodily fear,
    Had leap'd down from the wall to the floor.

All was silent again till a Dulcimer snored,
    Lack-a-day and what shall we hear next ;
A Jewtrump asks just but to utter a word,
    And he hopes that none here will be next.

Quoth an old Hurdy-gurdy he surely wont say,
    That he's one of the instrument class ;
If he does then a pipe made of straw too can play,
    And a tin penny whistle may pass.

Ye instruments all with my tongue in the mouth,
    Hums Jewtrump by all 'tis confess'd ;
Who understand music this evident truth,
    That the instrument's best that's played best,

The church clock struck two as I hurried home fast ;
    For it rain'd on my best sunday hat ;
And the sleepy police must have thought as I pass'd
    I was either a " sharp " or a " flat."

MORAL.

Let Phrenologists prate about skulls large and small
    And their bumps with their callipers span ;
But the bumps the best play'd on are chiefest of all,
    For the soul's the musician in man.

A SEQUEL TO SOUTHEY AND BYRON'S VISIONS OF JUDGEMENT.

——o——

Thus far no farther go was said to ocean,
    But not unto the spirit's venturous flight ;
Assist Urania for my heart's devotion
    Is ever thine. With me ascend the height

Spiritual—for I've got a daring notion,
　To sing of things beyond this solar light;
Pegasus trim thy wings, thy course is bent
Out of this dunghill earth,—man's transient settlement.

Gabriel was lounging on heaven's tower above,
　Smiling at Peter busy pennies summing;
And looking down the deep abyss he strove
　To guess the reason of a noisy coming
Tumult below—and spied a red thing move,
　Like rocket rising swiftly in the gloaming
Pursued by wild-fires—and he cried for love
　Of heaven Peter. "Whats the row down yonder?
Is hell's new engine running loose I wonder?"

On and enlarging came a horse of fire,
　With two young riders seated on his back,
Each holding in his grasp a harp whose wire
　Was finest Ophir gold. The reins lay slack
Upon the charger's neck which seem'd t' aspire
　To heaven's third story. After howl'd a pack
Of bloodhound critics, as hounds used to do
In old Virginia with two slaves in view.

Close fast the portals came a thunder hest,
　To make it faster Peter 'gainst it rear'd
His huge broad back—when to the spirits blest;
　An air of music came they listening heard,
Enchanted being unused to such a feast—
　(Yet of their carnal appetites afeared,)
For saints and angels are compelled to sing,
Nought but th' "Old hundred" and "My God the spring."

Saint Peter stood their passage to dispute,
　And as when parched Arabs reach a spring
Of water sweet, so angels drank each note;
　Like idiots gazing at the equine thing.
And all their pious duties quite forgot,
　Delighted to hear such charming ditties ring
On the high ramparts, cherub sentries shared;
The faults of mortals being off their guard.

Full on the gate they came then curb'd their steed,
　Rampant unbroke to stay careering loth
And both dismounted—loosing him to feed—
　And as wayfaring men oppress'd with drouth
And hunger, of some rest have sternest need:
　Knock at an Inn, so boldly knock'd they both,
When Peter through the gate ask'd who they were,

From whence they were, and what their business there.

The bolder whose fine eyes and ample brow,
  And noble bearing show'd him born as one
To rule replied. "We are well known below
  To some whose actions fear'd the mid-day sun.
Byron and Shelley English bards, and now
  Request protection—for yon hunter's dun
Are hard upon us—Kind Sir do be civil,
Unlock the door and save us from the devil."

I think I've heard some verses which you penn'd
  On Southey—Peter grunted—But you've stole
Look you; one of Satan's wildest horses friend;
  *Of that seen in th' Apocalypse the foal,
That feeds on meteors—and oft makes an end
  Of worlds!—and which will suffer no control
But his—I marvel how you caught and sat him,
For neither saint nor angel dare come at him.

At Missolonghi then quoth Byron, when
  I left my corse and wildly stared around,
At objects strange I spied this comet, then
  Oft wishing such a steed, I made a bound
And fairly strode him—some black ugly den
  I knew he stall'd in—where in woe profound,
'Mong smoke and soot with fiends in Hades belly,
I guess'd they'd thrust my timid friend poor Shelley.

Away, away Mazeppa flew no faster,
  Through Tartar wilds—I let him have his way,
He whisk'd his fiery tail and caused disaster
  To many a star—till at the shores of day;
He rear'd and kick'd, and tried to doff his master!
  At one sheer leap he clear'd the gulph which lay
Before him, and down Erebus we flew
Athwart the lake which Cain saw burn so blue.

Hands off Don Soot-bag, Peter harshly cried,
  As the Foulfiend was Shelley rudely seizing;
I'll draw my rusty weapon, yet a word
  From these two spirits; I know to thee displeasing.
Thou only art in thine own caverns lord,
  Keep off thy dogs. The story is amazing,
This fellow has commenced—in that I see
He has outrun, beat, and outwitted thee.

This said, Old Nick drew back his swarthy crew,
  The same that raced at Halloway kirk of old;
                    * Rev. vi, 8.

And Byron commenced again.   I said we flew
  O'er that blue lake which Cain saw and which roll'd
Its liquid fires as flames like tempest's blew,
  Fierce as norwesters sweep o'er Thule cold—
Nor stay'd my horse his speed till on a knoll
  Of lava hot I found poor Burns's soul.

Thou here I said, upon this barren coast,
  From banks of Ayr 'tis dismal here to dwell;
Ah! woe is me with groans return'd the ghost,
  All love—song-writers here are doom'd to hell.
For sneers at cant, and piety I'm lost;
  And Holy Willie is in heaven to swell
Its psalmody, with multitudes of others,
  Sav'd by the prayers and pious faith of brothers.

I crush'd an oath—my temper getting warm,
  And where's Rousseau, Voltaire, Goethe, Scott?
Dibdin, and shepherd Hogg, whose lyrics charm
  Millions—whose hearts ne'er knew a stain or spot,
All damned he sigh'd though never meaning harm,
  Does Campbell too partake their fiery lot;
Shakespear, Ben Johnson, Spencer, Dryden, Gay,
  Anacreon Hafiz, Petrarch of the ages grey,

Most of them are lost in Lethe's wave return'd
  The Scottish bard, or in lone places scatter'd—
And Shelley good shadow is he extra burn'd,
  Who certes never priest or preacher flattered;
I saw him by some canting spirits spurn'd,
  And almost into mince-meat bruised and batter'd
You'll find him on a pile of upas trees,
  Broil'd in the envenom'd shirt of Hercules.

So here you've brought him interrupted Peter,
  Could not the carnal fool have put the Psalms
In verse to some hymn tune of trumpet metre,
  Particular or common, or get palms
For hymns like Cowper—and then how much better
  Men's lives would be, when all their conscience qualms
Were hush'd, when every spirit was confided
  To priests and preachers,—heaven has always guided.

Crabb'd Peter softened by their tales of pain,
  Cough'd, expectorated then, and mused,
Then said to look for pennies were in vain,
  And though for love to ope the gates unused.
They might have entrance but he vow'd " Again,
  All spirits penniless would be refused;"

They might have fell'd the Poets with an apple,
When they walk'd through the gates into a chapel.

It was a mighty lovefeast and revival,
    One told how under him a sinner smarted,
Another had convinc'd a shopman rival ;
    A third from ruin's very brink had started,
A fourth for many years had striven to drive all
    Sinners to chapel ; and a fifth had parted
From a good friend, because he read a play,
A sixth had made his son love Sabbath day.

Angel, said Byron, to one near.   This clamour
    Is tiresome.   Who's yon man who looks so pure,
And beats the pulpit desk with fist for hammer,
    I think I've seen his countenance before,
He seems as if obsess'd with sacred glamour,
    Humph ! the angel answer'd, " Wesley to be sure,"
He was on earth the Methodistic leader,
And now in heaven their spiritual feeder.

And there stands happy Charles.   Once on a time
    He thought t' have joined heaven poets—but the guard
Soon as he heard his weak religious rhyme,
    The portals of the mansion double barr'd,
And told him that perhaps he still might climb
    Into that heaven, and get a wreath's award ;
So he return'd and join'd his brother John,
Who held that bards were *natus et non fit* alone.

Yonder among them too is little Watts,
    Not little minded—striving for a hearing,
But higher there, an ancient friend, why that's
    Southey, scream'd Byron, but they'll have no swearing,
Else—Silence, his guide imposed—Imbecile states
    Some fall into, when old age they are nearing—
But many hold his was sublime theocracy,
Others 'twas fear or avarice, or hypocrisy.

And now began a fervour past belief,
    Great Whitfield wheel'd around and cried—all those
Who love the Lord, be instant and not brief
    In prayer—When all the congregation rose
Each striving in devotion to be chief ;
    Some tumbled o'er the pews on others toes,
Some sang, some crack'd their voices, no one slept,
And many bent their heads and sigh'd, and groan'd, and wept,

Quoth Byron: Vulgar worship but sincere—
    Southey I envy not.   But let us go,

If their eternal happiness is here,
   Dear Cicerone mine is *not* I trow—
Then come along the guide said. We go where
   There is a place more suitable for you ;
For in my Father's house are mansions many,
To man declar'd, but not believed by any.

He led them to a place so glorious that they
   Were dazzled. Banquets for gods and wines of ruby red,
Bards and musicians and th' Elysian lay,
   And star crown'd beauty wonderous dances sped.
Song birds,—flowers of heavenly hues ;—and Joy was fed
   In groves and palaces. The guide then said—
Stay, an ye list for mansions still more gay,   [away.
If worthy you will find. Adieu! my friends, my mission calls

WHY LOOK WE BACK TO FADED BLOOMS?

Here is something quaint and rare ; we should dearly like to have a book full of such verses ; for they remind us of those staunch sons of song, Samuel Daniel George Herb rt, Robert Herrick, and the never-to be-forgotten George With r. How strangely they sound, in this grasping, money-loving age!—SPICE I LANDS.

Why look we back to faded blooms,
   And forms that may not stay ;
And mourn beside the moss-grown tombs
   Of objects pass'd away ?
Why care we for long bygone years,
   By foolish sorrow led ?
For in that vale the spirit hears
   But wailings for the dead.

'Tis in the future prospect we
   Shall find our peace of mind,
Dark is the mortal's destiny
   Who fondly looks behind :
Then on, then on, our lov'd ones live
   Where life's bright rivers flow ;
And if they grieve at all, they grieve
   That we stay long below.

With them, cold winter long has pass'd,
   Their strife is at an end ;
For ever hush'd the angry blast
   That made them shrink and bend.
Upon their brows, no shadows now

Bespeak the troubled mind;
Woe, want, and pain they left below—
  With us who stay behind.

"The winter's past, the clouds are gone,"
  I heard a lov'd one say:
"The turtle's voice cries, hasten on,
  "Come, brother, come away;
"Our vines give out a pleasant swell,
  "We've trimm'd our olive bowers,
"Bright garments here will fit thee well,
  "We'll crown thy head with flowers.

"Pine not for grandeur's earthly shoon,
  "Its hopes or pleasures gay;
"We, too, its best delights have seen:
  "Come, mourner, come away,
"Arise, arise, from earth arise!
  "Let fame unheeded call,
"And leave behind its poisoned skies;
  "For death has tainted all.

"We've fill'd a flagon high for thee;
  "For thee adorn'd a home;
"Where festive joy will ever be:
  "Come, lingering brother, come."
I come, I come, time's tardy pace,
  With song's I will beguile;
I soon shall end earth's weary race:
  Blest spirits, wait awhile.

THE MALE COQUETTE.

——:o:——

THERE was music from the orchestra, and perfume from the
  vase,
And ringing laughs and wit's retorts, and costly silks and lace,
There were jewels bright of starry sheen, and eyes more bright
  than they,
And light hearts. Were they light! at least the faces all were
  gay,
Carnation tinted many cheeks doom'd soon to fade and fly.
For falsehood and hypocrisy is ever ever nigh;

The boyant step, the graceful mien, the quick and roguish
   glance
Show'd amourous hope's fond luxury was mingled with the
   dance.
But there sat one whose sunny bloom had made an angel vain,
Ere love so foundly nurs'd had chang'd the joy of youth to pain,
She sat alone, and smiled not, spoke not—look'd with vacant
   eye,
As one in trance communing with the shades of things gone by,
Quick glances oft were shot on her; then lightly turn'd away,
As from a blighted ruin'd thing fast hastening to decay;
And one look'd oft, yet did not dream that wreck was made by
   him,
Who oft in other days had praised those eyes now growing dim.
Who once had villainously won a heart not cared to win,
And lit a flame that now consumed the vital part within,
His step was light with one as bright, as e'er gave lover pride,
His own his cherish'd maid, and now his bless'd affianced bride.
The ball was o'er, the lights were gone, and in a chamber lone
A lovely form was fainting, and her ailing all unknown;
And tearful eyes soon saw a dark funereal cortege move,
With a victim of male coquetry, of base unhallow'd love.

~~~~~~~~~~~~~~~~~~~~~~~~~~~~~~~~~~~~~~

FATHERLAND.

——:o:——

This world I know is not my home,
   'Tis but a caravanserail,
Where pilgrims fear the ills to come,
   Where mirage cheats and fountains fail,
'Mong alien wanderers I roam,
   A charnel path, a desert strand,
This weary world is not my home,
   My home* is in the Fatherland.

Here Chaldea's temples proudly shine,
   Here sons of God in sorrow bow;
Here Mammon's slaves in wealth repine,
   And care corrodes the jewell'd brow.
My heart disdains this earthly home,
   For where is all that youthful band,

  * Because man goeth to his long home.—Eccl. xii, 5.

That sported in a shortliv'd bloom—
   Gone, gone to happy Fatherland.

This tenement I like not now,
   'Tis old and falling to decay ;
The transient beauty once it wore,
   Wore with the dark brown years away.
A stranger now, I have no home,
   Though friendships cheer and smiles are bland,
I anxiously the hours consume,
   In thinking of my Fatherland.

My blood grows cold and nature cold,
   Attracts me less from day to day ;
The stars and sun seem waxing old,
   As I grow weary, old, and grey.
Heartless a wintry waste I tread,
   Whilst this old cabin's pillars stand,
Cheer'd only by the glimpses shed,
   From glorious realms of Fatherland.

THE TEMPTATIONS OF ST. ANTHONY, THE FIRST CATHOLIC MONK.

* Enimvero malum est videre fœminam, pejus alloqui, pessimum attingere.

Saint Anthony great in the annals of fame,
From Egypt his natal to Lebanon came,
The first of the Monachs, the anti uxorian,
The eremite pious, as states the historian.
Black, naked and filthy, and ugly and fat,
And holy and lazy he laid on his mat.

One morn as he sat in his stalactite cave,
Intent on his soul from the tempter to save,
A widow came tripping he knew not from whence,
But he felt most unable to spurn her from thence.
He felt as men feel who do nothing but pray,
But the demon of wedding will never heed Nay.

But he fought the fair temptress like anchorite brave,
While she wash'd up his vessels and clean'd up his cave,
She greased all his body with witchery's grace,
And lav'd with spring water his feet and his face,
Then she plump'd down beside him (O henious sin)
And chuck'd him (Oh, impudence !) under the chin.

* Yes it is bad to see a woman—worse to speak to one—and worst to touch one.—Catholic Legends.

Oh, widow ! O chastity ! how his mouth water'd,
The temptress was clever, but little it matter'd,
He growl'd like a dog that has got a sore head,
He bade her desist, but she would not be said.
For she begg'd and she pray'd of the hermit to try
To find out some sand she had got in her eye.
But still he resisted and fell on his knees,
Kiss'd his cross and his relic and by them got ease.

But virtue is weak in the world and the flesh,
And the temptress attacked him more closely afresh ;
Confections she brought, and Aleppo's red wine,
That smack'd as if fit for St. Benedict's shrine.
But still he held out till her arts being spent,
She kiss'd him (O shame) begg'd his blessing and went.

Deeply musing,—his ideas on penances ran,
He felt like an angel reduced to a man ;
And wept till he look'd upon Lebanon's snow,
That shone on the vine cover'd valleys below.
And to cool sinful blood in his veins boiling hot,
A heap for his bed in his grotto he got.

Asleep in the morn in the snows of his bed,
The brisk widow found him and instantly fled ;
By the miracle vanquish'd she shiver'd with cold,
And the fame thereof went through the churches of old.
'Tis said when he afterwards travelled through Nice,
With a look one grass widow he froze into ice,
And since his time, widows have trembled and shrunk
Half frozen when kissing the frock of a monk.

THE GHOST OF REUBEN HOLDER
APOSTROPHIZED.

——:o:——

Reuben Holder was a weak minded person, who some years ago almost daily vended his own silly doggerel Teetotal Rhymes in the streets of Bradford, and was actually believed by hundreds to be inspired.

Rest thee in peace great shade of Reuben Holder,
  Why still obsess our Bradford poet brood
We only laugh'd and often deem'd thee bolder
  Than most men,—climbing with thy cumb'rous load

Of fusty wit Parnassus' mountain. Colder
  To thee poor fellow than the world allow'd.
Is it dear ghost for past or present crimes,
That even yet thou pourest out thy rhymes.

Or is thy gloomy sprite migratory,
  As Gymnosophists teach in lore Brahminical,
Filling with jargous rhyme of Purgatory,
  The obsess'd souls of other poets finical.
Like thee agog, for tanners and for glory,—
  Peace Reuben—for we would not now be cynical,—
Could not the Faculty invent a good brain-wash,
For persons unaware that pen thy trash.

Yet Reuben thou wert harmless. Thou didst prattle
  Of things that rang'd within thy comprehension,
Far was't from thee with intellect to battle,
  For thine was small in thy titlark ascension.
But now thy spirit comes forth with a rattle,
  From spirits in thy demonized retention.
Good Tennyson hold fast thy laureate crown,
Or Reuben's ghost may sieze it as is own.

~~~~~~

SONNET.

A night scene in the Bay of New York, on the 4th of July; the Anniversary of the American Declaration of Independence.

The sky seem'd bronze—stars faint—upheav'd in east
  The blood-red moon. We anchor'd in the Bay,
Intense the heat. The dun hills went to rest
  By firefly lamps. A barge beside us lay
Like a black phantom. Sullen moan'd the sea
  Wild music charm'd its waters from the drum,
The trumpet and the gong. Continually
  The city threw up rockets. Through the gloom
Boom'd heavy cannon. Thick'ning clouds o'erspread,
  Roll'd their responsive thunders. Lightenings shook
Their quivering darts incessantly o'erhead,
  Our vessel roll'd. The welkin seem'd to rock,—
White flashes whisk'd about—then dropp'd big rain—
  And howling like a demon came the hurricane.

THE POOR MAN'S CHILD.

——:o:——

LITTLE traveller of earth !
No one smiles upon thy birth ;
Rudely thy weak limbs they bind,
And rough the swaddling clothes they find :
The wind screams through the cottage wild,
Cold welcome to the poor man's child !

Prattler on thy mother's knee !
Nursed with milk of misery ;
With plaintive songs she makes thee sleep,
And then her eyes have time to weep,
As musing o'er the woes up-pil'd,
Thou hast to bear, thou poor man's child !

She sees thee dash'd to earth with wrong,
With rags and shame thy mates among ;
She sees thy youth in mills immured,
Thy manhood unto toils inured ;
Thine age dishonoured and reviled,
Thy death unmourn'd, thou poor man's child !

Beside thy crazy cradle kneeling,
Rapt with all a mother's feeling,
She would pray, yet dares not pray,
That God would take her child away ;
And then recoils at thoughts so wild,
And feels she cannot spare her child !

And where is he in sweat and toil,
With hunger lank in shop or soil ?
Dear to his soul art thou at home,
Yet half he'd wish thou hadst not come—
Thy father ; are his cares beguiled ?
Ah, no ! they'r doubled by his child !

Go, get thee gone, sweet sleeper, hence !
Thou bursting bud of innocence ;
Go to angelic choirs, although
It were heart grief to see thee go ;
For grisly want and winter wild
Have met thy coming, poor man's child !

SONG.

——:o:——

Is not yon the lark's sweet voice, in
Azure mansions, lost in light?
Is not you the dove rejoicing
That she's 'scaped the winter night?

Welcome sunbeam, welcome flower,
Welcome ploughboy to the plain,
Welcome bird to budding bower,
Welcome spring-tide back again.

Come, my Betsy, let us rove on
Sunward banks where snowdrops thrive;
Don thy kirtle, haste, my lov'd one,
Joy and spring again revive.

Earth from her full casket's flinging
Gems of every radiant hue,
Her full choir of music bringing
To excite our songs anew!

SUNDAY MORN.

——:o:——

When the six day's toils are o'er,
And worldly cares distract no more;
When from forgetfulness we leap,
Refresh'd with rest and balmy sleep.
Where is the man by labour worn,
Who welcomes not a Sunday morn?

Gives not the sun a brighter beam?
Hums not more musical the stream?
Blow not the flowers in fairer light,
With lenses hung of colours bright?
While balmy gusts o'er meadows borne,
Smell sweeter on a Sunday morn.

How blest is he whose temp'rate head,
Through life by honest motives led;
With him are peace and plenty found,

His wife and children flourish round,
And roaming over dale and down,
Their heavenly Father's mercies own.

The drunkard's home how different,
His goods in pawn—his money spent,
His hopeless wife, and children weep
The tears of want—and he asleep
Till devils blue, rouse and affright
His senses in the Sunday light.

Pride the painted butterfly,
Another curse of poverty,
Inherits oft a kindred doom ;
Rich abroad and poor at home,
Outward show and debt's despair,
Fashion's cost and Sunday's care.

THE DETHRONEMENT OF KING CONSCIENCE.

——:o:——

PICKING his teeth with dogg'd and surly look,
Sat Sathanas and scowl'd at those about
Who had not knelt and kiss'd his cloven foot;
Then rose and to his lords in Council spoke.

"Ye beastly lazy knaves," said he ; for he
In Cromwell fashion rul'd his parliament,
" Here ye will lurk as quiet and content
As if ye could not work iniquity.

"Yonder king Conscience lords it o'er the world,
And makes it unto man a paradise ;
He gives all honour to the good and wise,
And in my face mine every gift is hurl'd ;

" He drives my daughter Sin to lonely places,
Afraid to show her face so sweet and fair.
My occupation's gone—Mars keeps his lair—
And harmony and peace man's mind debases.

" Stir thee, brass talon'd Mammon, get thee up,
Or I shall soon be forc'd to shut up shop ;
Thy grave-like maw is not yet full, I hope :
  Arise ! and on the earth, ere sunset, sup.

H

" And take with thee that precious yellow metal,
Which I have found a magnet to the souls
Of fools ; for we must rule the earth by fools,
Or Angels 'mong the sons of men may settle."

Growling, grim Mammon rose, and took his hoard,
Put on man's shape—but could not change his eye
Of fascinating greed—assay'd to fly,
While the Divan with hideous laughter roar'd.

Conscience was busy comforting the sad,
The aged, and infirm (when Mammon rose)
And hospitably to his worst of foes,
Thinking no evil, wide his doors display'd.

" What waste is this," says Mammon to the court
Of royal Conscience, " see how poor you'r grown—
Hold, hold your hands, and let not every clown
Be equal with you—you're a tyrant's sport.

Obey not Conscience men—see here this gold
'1 will bring you more than Conscience ever gave—
Your king makes each far worse than any slave :
He's but a slave and may be bought and sold."

Struck with th' audacious speech—the king beheld
Sin just behind th' intruder—and exclaim'd,
" Turn out the wretch, or we're for ever sham'd ;"
But nearly all, by (Mammon led,) rebell'd.

All was confusion—some of spirits stout
By Conscience stood, whom they'd lov'd well and long ;
But those on Mammon's side were much too strong
For Conscience and his friends, whom they thrust out.

PSALM CXXXVII. VERSIFIED.

——:o:——

WE sat and wept by Babel's streams,
    Our harps on willows hung ;
They ask'd for mirth—who wasted us,
    For songs in Zion sung.

How could we for our taunting foes—
    A mournful captive band—
Sing Zion's songs in Babylon,
    And on a foreign strand,

Lov'd Salem! may its cunning all
　From my right hand depart,
When fades in regal loveliness
　Thine image from my heart.

And let my tuneless tongue unto
　My palate cleave, when I
Prefer not fair Jerusalem
　Above my chiefest joy,

Remember cruel Edom's hate,
　O, God! in Zion's day,
Who wish'd her walls foundationless,
　And we far, far away.

And thou shalt sink thou harlot queen—
　Thou river dragon red;
Aad happy he who visiteth
　Our woes upon thy head.

Yea, blessed he who 'gainst the stones
　Shall dash thy serpent brood;
And Baal in his Babylon
　Drown in Assyrian blood.

THE SPECIAL CONSTABLE.

——:o:——

What I'm going to relate is most certainly true,
　(Stand back or I'll give you a lick),
Your hearts, stars, and garters, you'd bless if you knew
　All about my miraculous stick.

First and foremost, while taking it out in my hand
　When Fenians were "mould" for a riot;
They spied my approach, and began to disband
　For they saw they had better be quiet.

The wonders it did in the country appeared
　In the papers—its manling wild mobs;
Its knocking down drunkards and other absurd
　Poor people, but missing the *nobs.*

News ran and news spread through the country side quick
　As scandal—and letters I got

By dozens, requesting to borrow my stick
    To bang burglars, dogs, wives, and what not.

'Tis said it was made by old daddy John Bull,
    When his chattels were going to pot ;
And the guess of a nation is never so dull
    When 'tis getting it *Specially* hot.

One day with old dad's constitutional prop,
    I met with the Mayor, d'ye see ;
And as soon as my truncheon he twigg'd, a full stop,
    He made, and a genteel *congee.*

Then the Vicar came up, and he gazed and he gazed,
    Till I thought the man must be a flat,
For he stared at my stick like a howlet amazed,
    Then politely he lifted his hat.

The ladies turn'd pale, and the ladies turn'd red,
    Till I thought the sweet doves would turn sick ;
And they curtseyed and whispered, but oft I heard said,
    " Smart gent, " and " miraculous stick."

Some say that my stick is the old crab-tree staff
    Wherewith Balaam belaboured his ass ;
As to asses, 'tis true, but I smother a laugh,
    At the jolternowl's fears as I pass.

'Tis whispered my stick never grew in a bower
    On earth ; that some genius of evil
Has stole it, filled full of strange mesmeric power,
    From the witch faggot pile of the d—l.

The Bradford Town Council's wise Solomons met
    Last week, and by placard made known
That in cases of peril my stick they must get
    To defend the police of the town.

So, look'ee, my lads, if ye fight, aye, or wag
    A finger, your noddles I'll rattle ;
For my stick is a chunk of the staff of the flag
    That so long braved the breeze and the battle.

Move on, now my hearties, come nudge on ahead
    (Ods bodikins, bludgeons, and groans) ;
If any chap dares to dispute what I've said
    I will fill his skin full of sore bones.

THE SWANS.

The feathered subjects of the following lines were the property of Mr. Whitaker, of the Vale of Todmorden, son of Dr. Whitaker, the celebrated topographer and historian.

AMONG green mountains unrenown'd,
  (Truth sanctifies my song)
Two stately snow-white swans were found
  That lov'd each other long.

Still side by side with tall necks bow'd,
  Still to each other true.
Like emperor and empress proud,
  They skimmed the waters blue.

The sun that sunk behind the hill
  Still left their hearts allied,
And up with crimson morning still
  Smiled on them side by side.

A lady pass'd and saw such love
  As man could ne'er maintain,
And sighed that human love should prove
  In contrast light and vain.

Rude hands destroy'd the noble male,
  And his mate no more will fly,
As sometimes was their wont, the vale,
  And wing the mountain sky.

No power can make her now forsake
  The green her partner trod:
She sails where he sail'd on the lake,
  Sits on the same dear sod.

Low moonlight strains by lake and stream,
  Charm lovers as they stray;
That 'tis the swan they little dream,
  That sings her life away.

The lady pass'd and view'd again
  The widow'd swan's distress,
And sigh'd " No more boast, woman vain,
  Thy truth and faithfulness."

A WIFE AND FRIEND.

THERE are two gems of princely worth,
  Two amulets for pain;

That give true courage on the earth,
　　Our trials to sustain.

One is a wife to take our fate,
　　And stereotyp'd to smile;
The other is a friend and mate,
　　The teeth of care to file.

The gain of both is wisdom's end,
　　And trial soon will prove;
That friendliness will find a friend,
　　A loving spirit love.

These won how light through toil and strife,
　　Life's pendulum will go;
From friendly cheer to bosom dear,
　　Returning to and fro.

Though wife may die our friend is nigh,
　　Of both we're not bereft;
Though friend be gone we're not alone,
　　We have one comfort left.

THE BESOM HAWKERS.

————:o:————

Some time agone, in Bradford's busy fair,
A witty rogue cried besoms everywhere:
" Six for fourpence only!　Here's your sort!
Ladies use them up at court.
View them o'er and trust your eyes,—
Got the Exhibition prize!
Handle right and when you please—
Like old Van Scamp— you'll sweep the seas.
Besoms new, all tight and true,
Come buy, my pretty dears, come buy!
Here's a bargain—sweep and try.
I mean to sweep on this occasion
All besom rogues out of the nation:
Church and House of Commons too,
I'll give a sweeping through and through.
Half-a-dozen for a groat,
Fit to brush your Sunday coat!
Mary Ann, love, pick them out,—

Selling off for next to nought ;
Mountain beauties, four for six,
Pinwire heather, whalebone sticks—
Take me, darlings, while you may,
Never trust another day."
A fellow besom hawker standing by,
Driven from the market by his cry,
Call'd him aside, and thus began :
" Comrade, I cannot comprehend your plan ;
I prigs my steyls and ling, and every rap,
That's used by any besom making chap.
I'll stand a handsome treat if you will tell me
The reason why you still can undersell me,"
" Come on," cheap Joe replied ; and trigg'd his tripes
With mutton chops and double X for swipes ;
Then looking sly, he wink'd his eye and said,
" Matey ! I prigs my besoms ready made !"

THE EMIGRANTS.

———o———

ADIEU, thou dear land of our birth,
The exiles of England we mourn ;
The half-famish'd swallow will leave thee in dearth,
And return with the summer to plenty and mirth,
But we go and we never return.

Thou hast look'd on our childhood with care,
And may blessings for aye o'er thee flow ;
But the hopes that we cherish'd all melted in air,
And the blackness came down of the night of despair,
Dear Mother and from thee we go ;

All hail ye white waves of the main,
Like a bird shall our bark o'er ye fly,
With her white wings abroad on the dark azure plain ;
The toy of the storm, in his own vast domain
The plaything for winds of the sky.

The huge swelling billows may heave,
But we fear not their deep hollow roar ;
Our minds wander back and their terrors decieve,
To our friends kindred loves, and oh sadly we grieve ;
For that hearth we revisit no more.

The depths of the forest shall be

By Canadas rivers our home ;
Where the nightly wolf howls 'neath the dark hemlock tree,
And the fell panther prowls, and the nimble deer flee
Through the cedar swamps terrible gloom.

Though the serpent glares fierce on us there,
By the shanty our home shall arise ;
Where the red hunter rests, its frail walls we will rear,
And his Manitous haunt shall our axes lay bare
To the warm cheerful light of the skies.

Rich harvests our children shall have,
Where the whippoorwill nightly calls now ;
And great cities rise of the free and the brave,
And Commerce, her banners in ev'ry port wave,
With the myrtle of peace on her brow.

A CHAUNT.

——:0:——

In a second hand coat and a hat for a groat,
Respectable is my turn out ;
I travel along ever crooning a song,
Of the way of the great I get out.

What now do I care for the gay or the fair,
If sad or if merry they be ;
For the Muse with a smile often comes to beguile,
With her treasures, the moments to me.

The valleys of bloom, and the gales of perfume,
The songs and the jewels of spring ;
With my youth have long gone, yet my spirit lives on,
And I know I shall cease not to sing.

I have seen the untruth of romances of youth,
While his furrows Time plough'd on my face ;
But I've strove for the right, I have fought the good fight,
To the poor I have been no disgrace.

The gods saw my fate and in pity take that,
They said and they gave me the string ;
Fickle Fortune may frown, and enjoyments be gone,
But of better days coming I'll sing.

There are meads we can roam round a ready* "long home,"
From this body's clay cottage I ken :

*" Because man goeth to his long home." Eccles. xii. 5.

Where no " Notice " is given no tenant is driven,
From his dwelling by insolent men.

It is there we can stray even here while we stay,
On aquiline pinions we fly;
And look down upon earth as a place of no worth,
A lazar house, bedlam, or stye.

The woes that began ere my years reach'd the man,
The dread future ever hung o'er;
And the old horrid glare of want woe and despair,
Shall affright and distress me no more.

In a beautiful strand a delectable land,
Love reigns as a Parent and king;
Where each sense is a feast—all cares are at rest,
Each heart throb impels them to sing.

My time I abide for mortality's pride
Evanescent and transcient I know;
And in many a lay hearty homage I'll pay,
On the harp to my king as I go.

IMPUDENCE.

——:o:——

WERE'T not that loss of character I hate,
Thou wicked woman I would break thy pate.

Ovid.

Ere heavenly Venus lov'd the Dardan boy,
Or Juno's Argives first invested troy;
Ere Ate blighted silver Simoian bowers,
Or Mars was heard from Illium's topmast towers.
Long ere Arachne falsehood's tissue wove,
And scorn'd Palladian webs of truth above;
Ere Mercury in sleep shut Argus eyes,
And vomited Deucalion's flood of lies.
The world in youth—when cloud compelling **Jove,**
Was feasting in a bright Hesperian grove;
Her golden cestus lovely Venus wore,
And shield and helmet proud Minerva bore.
Loud laughter rung—Appolline music flow'd,—
And godesses and gods dane'd in a crowd,—
Hebe had fill'd Jove ruby cup,—when lo!
Who should arrive but Hermes on tiptoe,

And bowing low in mock obeisance stood;
Grinning and smirking much unlike a god.
" How now, Quoth Jupiter! what brings you here?
You half-bred jackanapes with roguish leer, "—
And grasp'd his thunder—Hermes turning pale,
Show'd more respect and then commenc'd his tale.
" Brave fiddling here with harlots all arow,
Regardless of poor mortals down below,
Listen tho uproar—Masses of mankind;
The ignorant and brainless you will find
Are perishing—The sensible and wise
Live and get fat—It would not cause surprise
If things go on"—"Come skipjack that will do
Snapp'd Jupiter—I see thy meaning through,—
I can't be always minding things below;
Can I fair Dian with thy silver bow ?"
He turn'd upon her an inquiring look ;—
She smiled on Mercury and ere she spoke,
Into her Hecate nature turned the maid ;
(While near Jove's throne ran Ganymede afraid,)
Then answer'd—Mighty Thunderer, if still"
You love me, let Caduceus have his will ;—
Jove scratch'd his lock's ambrosial—starsnuff—took,
Then to Caduceus again he spoke,
To spoil my pastime you may find no joke.—
Begone and quickly ere thy pate is broke—
Come next at proper seasons, ugly thief,
When I in judgment sit,— and then be brief—
Cet out—and when you find men scant of sense,
Give for amends a stock of impudence.
Mercury fled and often look'd behind,
In fear for rolling thunder in the wind ;
Then probity and sense became the jest.
Of ladies fine—and impudence was blest,—
The gods were mock'd. The iron age began,
And old relations chang'd of man to man.

~~~~~~~~~~~~~~~~~~~

TITTER UP TACK'T.*

——:o:——

Tom-mee, Sam-mee, honies get up,
  T' craw's driving t' starlins ta t' skoil,

*Soonest up take it.

T' dogs foit's in his pocket sin t' battle with t' tup,
 T' cats' comein her toppin ot' stoil.
Ye're just like two hullots it' toithwark it' lair,
 While t' gobblecock's flytin his dame;
I'll ta bed an out war ya young urchans, d'ye hear,
 T' larks shahwtin dahwn chinla for shame.

SINGS.

There was a young widow I cannot say where,
 And she went a walking to take the fresh air;
She met a young parson just coming that way,
 " Good morning" how are you? sweet blossom **of May.**
Come out for fresh air in the meadows I ween—
 Your sweetness makes sweeter the breath of the bean;
Neck and crop love has bound me in fetters, said he,
 And what said the widow? why nothing said she!
Derry down, &c.

Tom-mee Sam-mee. Father's it' hagg
 Threng turnin ower t' rigwalted muggs;
If a comes wi' that saplin he split off a t' snag,
 He'll welt both yer shoothers an lugs.
There's t' bull emeng t' beepiches tail up it' air,
 They'll teych common sense ta sich tykes;
I've set t' clockin hen, an I've fother'd grey **mare,**
 Wal ye lig like two paddocks it' sykes.

SINGS.

My trade is a good one. I've tithe pigs to eat,
 And wine from the parish my cronies to treat;
With nobles and gentles I dine and I ride,
 Tantivy a hunting at Martinmass tide.
So wilt thou be mine pretty widow, said he,
 And what said the widow? a bargain said she;
And 'twere only fairplay all the parish would own,
 That I wear the breeches, while you wear the **gown.**
Derry down, &c.

Tom-mee, Sam-mee, t sen's burning off t' thack,
 Two piuats are threaping wit' pig;
I been dahwn a milkin ta t' coppy an back,
 Haw long are ye both bahwn ta lig.
It's skoil time—ye'd gawm ma ma more ner a **dunnock,**
 If t' clack o' me thropple I crackt;
But I'll stir ye I lay—Here's a nice treacle **bunnock,**
 Da ya hear ma lads? Titter up tack't!

GOD IS LOVE, 1. John, 4. 16.

—:o:—

WHERE the heart's ease grew and the halcyon flew,
  And the vines with the roses wove ;
On eternity's throne with the sun for his crown,
  In his beauty and power sat Love.

He was king of the east, he was king of the west,
  He was Lord of the mountain and flood ;
And the pure and the fair to adore him came near,
  From the castle and merry greenwood.

To His glimmering court kings and queens made resort
  His majesty's grace to behold ;
On His right hand was Truth on His left hand youth,
  Clad in heaven wrought azure and gold.

His armies abroad on the hurricane rode,
  He commanded His ministers mild ;
And the leopard became, at His countenance tame,
  And the lion was led by the child.

At His opening spring, human winter took wing,
  With his fierce legions riding afar ;
And the hero of fame and the conquerer came,
  Treading down their blood-laurels of war.

The admiral brave left his fleet on the wave,
  That made hideous the watches of night ;
And he sat in the grove, with the children of Love,
  At the banquet of fruits of delight.

His pavilions heard the good news of His Word,
  And the sound of His harps never ceas'd ;
And the turnings of years and the burnings of spheres,
  Saw no end to His revelry blest.

THE OWL AND BIRDS OF NIGHT.

A Fable.

For every one that doeth evil, hateth the light. John 3 20,

It was upon a gloomy night,
When ghosts were flitting fleet ;
To Bolton's Abbey ruined quiet,

The nightbirds wing'd their gloomy flight,
In conference to meet.

On wall shrubs round sat many a fowl,
And on a broken slab ;
His mossgrown platform stood the owl,
And with great gravity, the whole,
Address'd with learned gab.

(Who-hoo) My friends you all (who-hoo)
Delight in chick like me ;
The good dame is our ancient foe,
And we have all a right you know,
To chicks as good as she.

I stole a leveret from the park,
A turkey from the green,
And a fat plump duckling in the dark ;
Had it been light, the certain mark
Of deadly gun I'd been.

I am for union—Foes unknown,
Sent eagle down to say,
Our wicked deeds love gloom alone,
And that we ought to face the sun
And catch our food by day ;

Sage men like owls love mystery all,
And some call darkness light ;
In gloom we all see best—To call
Thick darkness light is natural,
And nature dictates right.

Nature gave all for self to long,
And fear of light to feel ;
Nature says " steal "—evade the wrong
Nam'd justice—" and all things among—
Has nature's voice cried " steal "

Nights' shroud alone I for my part,
Have ever lov'd to view ;
I heard indeed the proud upstart,
And wish'd my talons in his heart,
How say my friends (who-hoo)

Squire Owl thou hast both sense and nerve,
Scream'd all the night birds then ;
The rogue would wish us all to starve,
But we by hab or nab will carve,
As crat for cock and hen.

Then hurried out the filthy rout,
(As loudly crow'd the cock)
The eagles power to set at nought ;
And tear his lofty eyrie out,
Though founded on a rock.

And as they wing'd with c' .nging cries,
Of threat and hate and sco.n ;
To their great terror and surprise,
Wide opened in the orient skies
The eyelids of the morn.

MORAL.

Few seek for witnesses of all they do,
And fortune's lovers are exposed to few ;
Evil, desires concealment, clouds, and night,
But good rejoices in the morning light.

SONG. FANNY AND ANNIE.

——:o:——

I lov'd both my Fanny and Annie,
 I am cert.in I lov'd them too well ;
But whether sweet Annie or Fanny,
 To chose I was bother'd to tell.

If I were to marry with Annie,
 I fear'd that poor Fanny would die ;
I could not be cruel to Fanny,
 The fact was I never could try.

I dallied long puzzled as either,
 To marry I felt I was loth ;
For I could be cruel to neither,
 And could not be married to both.

Like the ass and the hayricks in fable,
 Between them in choosing he died ;
So I in a fix was unable,
 To make up my mind if I tried.

And Fan grew as saucy as never,
 And suddenly gave me the sack ;
And Nan with a farewell for ever,
 Look'd haughty and sho.v'd me her back.

And Fanny got splic'd to a sailor,
    And sail'd with him over the sea,
And Annie got stitch'd to a tailor ;
    Was ever a lover like me ? hum !
Was ever a lover like me ?

SENTIMENTAL.

——:o:——

It is sweet when lord Titan from Thetis' bed rouses,
    And flings off his dusty old blanket the fog ;
To stray through the wild laughing pansies and roses—
    And suddenly squelch to the knees in a bog,

Cheering the bird and the balm of the morning,
    Celandines aureate by cascade and pool ;
The milkmaid to meet down the green lane returning,
    And hear her sweet greeting—"Gan on ya dazed fool !"

It is rich when reclined on the moss by the fountain,
    Its streams strewing gems on their crystalline way,
Cuckoos through rainbows awaking the mountain,—
    To be seized and for trespass have smartly to pay !

Rapture ! heaven's galaxys, myriad stars winking,
    Meteors in silence ablaze to behold,
To sit with Lucina, the pearly dew drinking—
    And catch rheum, mucus, cough, hoarseness, and cold !

To sup with the gods when Apollo, the warder
    Of Helicon's nectar-vaults, gives you a treat
Is glorious— with rent in arrear In your larder
    A ghost—for your family nothing to eat !

Bear witness ye wood-nymphs, ye dryads in scarlet,
    To joys all denied to the prosaic soul—
When your wife calls you lazy limbed, addle- brain'd varlet,
    And combs your elf-locks with a three-legg'd stool !

O solace for sorrow and happy abstraction,
    When storms in their caves Hyperborean doze !—
When you grope in your pockets and find not a fraction,
    And the Dule in your purse in his dancing shoes !

Charming to pour out your joy or your sorrow,
  Sympathy's cars by your lyrics to win,
And to send to the TIMES and perceive on the morrow—
  That the rascally Editor won't put it in!

<hr />

THE SPECTRE.

——:o:——

The following poem was suggested by the relations of spectral appearances to two seperate ladies, both of mature age, and both distinguished for their piety and love of truth.

THE clouds were dense on Ebor's skies,
And midnight thoughts took spectral guise
To lone affliction waking,
As hopeless in her vain employ ;
Lamenting for her buried boy,
A mother's heart was breaking.

She starts a well known call to hear
As soft as evening Zephyrs bear
A tongueless voice from heaven,
Mother it said ! awake ! behold
Thy son from Eden's hills of gold—
Thy spirit's veil is riven.

A form appear'd ! of heavenly mien,
Its raiment of a rosy shreen :
Its ruby lips still speaking,
" Forbear thy grief we do not die ;
We do not sleep and coldly lie
Entomb'd and unawaking."

"My home is bright I live and love
In Paradise— its spicy grove
In Spring's eternal blossom,"
Embolden'd with excess of joy,
One kiss she moan'd—one clasp my boy ;
Would heal thy mother's bosom.

The voice angelic spoke again,
" Thy lips would seek to kiss in vain,
" A lip belov'd so dearly
" But oft I'll leave my river's streams,

And clasp thee in thy morning dreams,
And kiss and ne'er be weary."

A sound as of a heavenly train,
Went with the light in sweet refrain,
To happy homes returning;
Some tears of joy the mother wept,
Laid down her head in peace, and slept,
And comfort crown'd the morning.

A CRIMEAN SONG.

——:o:——

AMONG the groves the linnet loves,
  About the time of spring;
One even clear I chanc'd to hear,
  A gentle lady sing.

I know a knight* of honour bright,
  Gone o'er the distant sea;
In arms, and chase, he'd not disgrace,
  The olden chivalry.

From sybil plan a talisman,
  My fingers for him wove;
And from my hands in other lands,
  He wears it for my love.

The gods of war may roar afar,
  In Crimean sulphur gloom;
To snowy skies, may soldiers cries,
  Bewail their island home.

In broken sleep may mothers weep,
  And maidens mourn in vain
For those who deep the carnage heap,
  In dyes of crimson stain.

But overruling Providence,
  And bands of angels near;
And stars benign will all combine,
  To guard my cavalier.

Beneath the summer's purple sky,
  The groves shall hear my swain
Repeat the love of days gone by,
  In Fountaindenn again.

* The Earl of Cardegan,

1

A MEMENTO VITÆ OF THE LATE EARL OF DERBY.

——:o:——

Imbued with the lore of the sage and the good,
  Wisdom's pathway he never forsook ;
And deeply in valley and mountain and flood,
  Nature's lessons he read in her book,
The beast and the bird and the blossom he lov'd ;
  When to strike the harp's chords he began,
From friendship and patronage genius prov'd
  That his head was the head of a man.

Affliction and poverty, hardship and pain,
  Had his earnest attention and care,
The spirit of freedom ne'er sought him in vain
  To protect it from " giant Despair."
He lit up with a smile ;—made the rainbow appear,
  On the face of the care-worn and wan ;
And many will cherish his memory dear,
  For his heart was the heart of a man.*

Like the law-giver Moses his bearing was meek,
  The peerage was marshall'd by him ;
He had led the Ephori the pride of the Greek,
  Roman Senate, or Jew's Sanhedrim,
From nobles descended true noble was he ;
  He sought Divine order in things ;
By nature created a noble was he,
  And a peer by the Monarch of kings.

HIC JACET.

——o——

A woman laid decently by,
  Some few have been worse and some better ;
She liv'd and she died so as long to defy,
  Man, woman, or child, to forget her.

Her love for her sex all her actions can tell,
  By tokens too many to mention ;
Her blacking-brush daily she handled so well,
  That no one escaped her attention.

* Lancashire cotton weavers remember him.

She was honest as sunshine when trusted with aught,
   Too distant, too hot, or too heavy ;
And if the bare truth she so often forgot,
   She lov'd it she swore on her davy.

She was call'd a foul witch by the tall and the small,
   A witch was she ? Was she a fiddle ?
And her tongue was not like a mill-hopper at all,
   Mill-hoppers dont hang by the middle.

She was cat-like they said—They say aught but their
    prayers,
   They say she lov'd slanderous story ;
But now what they said, very little she cares,
   For an arvil they said was her glory.

A husband she had, but the sensitive oaf,
   Felt her words like the spikes of a rowel ;
And he ne'er saw her want, for he bought her a loaf,
   Then hung himself up in a towel.

An infant she bore, and it crew and it grew,
   In beauty like every other ;
But it spread its soul wings and to heaven it flew,
   When it first took the stock of its mother.

Ere she tapp'd at death's door all her neighbours had oft,
   Appeal'd to their Maker together ;
To take her in mercy alow or aloft,
   For they were not particular whether.

A VISION.

——:o:——

Poor, wretched, half-starved in a garret I pined,
   By a grate with a handful of fire ;
There was night on the world, but the gloom of my mind
   Was deep'ning more awful and dire,
O whither to go—in what corner to hide ;
   From the world and the pomp of its insolent pride,
From the fears closing round me on every side,
   Not one way of escape though the world is so wide ;
Woe is me earth rejects me in wildness, I cried,
   And I wept all alone in my woe.

And ere I ceased weeping, exhausted I fell,
   From sheer want and fatigue into rest ;

And all I then saw I'm unable to tell,
  For I dreamt I had mix'd with the blest.
There was tuning of harps by high seraphic powers,
  And fairer than Enna in loveliest hours;
Were vistas of Edens and gardens of flowers,
  Living fountains, and regal pavilious and towers;
With rainbows around and above.

There were cities on mountains that shone as of gold,
  With foundation of jewels and light;
And I saw their high portals like lightning unfold,
  Whence issued the cherubim bright.
And a song as of myriads I heard as one choir,
  Attuned to the organ the viol and lyre;
From the east to the west like the rushing of fire,
  From the south to the north, where I heard it expire,
And the name of its burden was love."

I entered a mansion, whose adamine doors,
  Swung in music on hinges of gold;
Fiery columns arose from its opaline floors,
  And loves purple flames o'er it roll'd.
There were thrones (silver curtained from heavenly looms)
  Of soft yielding roses, in rich living blooms;
And Hygeian censers shed healing perfumes,
  And angels with smiles sang—" At length here he comes,
To the land of delight and content "

  Rich banquets of sweets in profusion were spread
With wine-cups that ever o'erflow;
  I tasted, and oh how delicious that bread
And that wine—there is none such below
  I tasted—new light seem'd to burst from the skies;
And the leaves of the olive, were chang'd into eyes,
  Fruits of life bent to kiss me with deep blushing dyes;
And the mountains began in the sheen to arise,
  For the wisdom of Life was the light.

Thrice happy are they who are dead in the Lord,
  For I seemed to the angels most dear;
They tenderly press'd to partake of their board,
  Officious my sorrows to cheer.
Their care is alone the sad sufferer to sooth,
  As in beauty immortal they bloom into youth;
Their words sounded soft as the winds of the south.
  Their features beamed innocence kindness and truth,
And their raiment will never grow old.

They directed mine eyes to the eastward on high,
And I fell down afraid and adored ;
For there zoned with glories of love in the sky,
I encountered the glance of the Lord.
Want and grief in the world have long caused me to bend,
But blessed is he who endures to the end ;
For I saw my Supporter, Redeemer, and Friend,
In that glance of the Vision Divine.

ODE TO THE DEMON OF INTEMPERANCE.

———:o:———

Intemperance is bad because it is not Temperance, and not
because it is not Teetoalism—therefore it has been called in, .
or untemperance, and not in or unabstinence.

These are the generations of Temperance and Intemperance.
God is the father of goodness ; Goodness is the father of
wisdom ; Wisdom is the father of reason ; Reason is the father
of Temperance ; Temperance is the father of long life and his
brethren, such as riches honour, &c.

The Devil is the father of evil ; Evil is the father of lies ;
a Lie is the father of Unreason ; Unreason is the father of Intemperance ; Intemperance is the father of total Abstinence—
ergo Intemperance, and total Abstinence have no kinship with
Temperance ; Temperance could never have begotten total
Abstinence.

Turkey the best fitted nation in the world for the cultivation
of the vine, has been sunk in ignorance and poverty since the
time of the Hegira, by the insane prohibition of the use of wine
by Mahomet. But for that her trade and commerce would have
been larger than that of France, and her civilization would
have kept pace with it. Her maritime and inland cities would
not have fallen to ruin. Her opiates would have been neglected
or totally unknown, except to her Mediciners, as in the West;
and her population would have gradually become infidels to her
false Allah, her Eblis, and her Mahound.

The fate of France, Spain, and Italy, would have been similar
to that of Turkey, under a similar political and religious prohibition.

"Now I say unto you, refrain from these men (Total
Abstainers) and let them alone ; for if their counsel or their

work be of men it will come to nought : but if it be of God
(i.e. founded upon truth for God is truth) ye cannot overthrow
it : lest haply ye be found to fight against God (i.e. Almighty
Truth)—ACTS v., 38, 39.

———

FROM what hell didst thou rise thus to vanquish the wise,
Thus to mildew the young and the fair ;
With hot irons to sear bosoms loving and dear,
And hoar age to o'erwhelm with despair.

From what nook of the pit, where the claw'd furies flit,
Didst thou bring thine intemperate bowl
Thou grim demon god, death and hell in thy trod,
Follow fast with their ministers foul.

Not the carnage deep red where the grave's maw is fed,
When the murder rife battle fields roar ;
When the skies blush for shame at the conqueror's name,
As he stalks through the black clotted gore.

No, not Mars nor the sea, when the winds are set free,
And when dark visaged hurricane's frown ;
When Neptune's green head is rear'd up from his bed,
And his trident strikes armadas down.

Not earthquakes that rend when the mountain's heads bend,
And affrighted streams fly to their source ;
When th' abyss's jaws grin and snatch proud cities in,
Nature seeming to swerve from her course.

Not contagions that fly through the poisoned sky,
When pestilence rages at worst ;
When putrid and blue corpses blast the sun's view,
And the bonds of affection are burst.

Not the pit, though it spue its black vomit and blue,
May we like thee Intemperance dread ;
For thy bright reaming bowl poisons body and soul,
It ferments in the vaults of the dead.

Bloated fiend, Scotland mourns, go and look o'er her urns,
With thy glassy and maniac glare ;
Old England weeps now for her brightest sons low,
Where are they ? bloated devil say " where?"

Where are millions, aye, where, who have tasted thy cheer,
By the bale-fires of Beelzebub brew'd ;
Thy red brazen brow shall protect thee not now,
Thou hast murder'd the great and the good.

Go and look at the cot of the maudlin sot,
Where the matron's tears freeze in her eyes ;
So cold, squalid and bare that a residence there
E'en a Hottentot's heart would despise.

The road to the gallows begins at thy palace,
The rope thou art spinning within—
There the prostitutes smile and mad passions beguile,
Gulphing fools to the pitfalls of sin.

Trace in dungeon's green slime thy confessions of crime,
While thy flesh sawing fetters cry clank ;
Where thy blasphemies pass to thy skies of hot brass,
And thy day star of hope is a blank.

Listen demon of doom to the thunders that boom,
Through the dark windy vault of the skies ;
With the driving hailcloud for the shriek long and loud,
Of distress on its pinions flies.

Let the streets tell the tale in the keen wintry gale,
Of the houseless and heart-broken wretch ;
Let the felon proclaim thy detestable name,
As he flings his last rag to Jack Ketch.

Go with thousands thou'st sent heavy chain'd to lament
Their crimes and their homes far away ;
The hulks know thy crimes and the antipode climes,
Of far Norfolk and Botany Bay.

Not Moloch the beast at his cannibal feast,
When the roast human members he shared ;
Not Belial the liar, were he sear'd with sky fire,
Would be with Intemperance compared.

Not the dread Juggernaut at his annual ride out,
When the screams of the Hindoos were hush'd ;
With the gong and tambour and the multitude's roar,
As the skulls of his victims were crush'd.

Not the witch fiend that mov'd our dark fathers, and lov'd
The faggot and roast living flesh ;
When match'd with thy rites where thy fiery snake bites,
Did they come from perdition afresh.

Off to doom to thy place with thy pock pimpled face,
Humanity's incubus black ;
And thy fiery thirst slake at the blue burning lake,
And look well that thou stagger'st not back.

Stop thy devils of blue let th' avenger pursue,
And with scorpion scourges thou'rt driven ;

Howling down to the deep, from thy heavy beast sleep,
Arous'd by the curses of heaven,

Nations ban thee dread power that the opening flower
And the promise of genius dost blight ;
That for patriot and bard has the madhouse prepared,
Shorn of energy, beauty, and might.

Stinking barrel-dreg, skunk, th' inside of thy trunk
Is a stagnant green reptile fill'd swamp ;
Gambling parasite, pimp, dirty hog, devils imp,
Ragamuffin, mean shovelling scamp.

Thine innocence gone and thy shame left alone,
Earth and heaven eternally lost ;
God and man made thy foes go and seek thy repose,
With the wild ghastly suicide host.

Apollyon ! away with thy dash and thy crash,
Brute's catches, jibes, swagger and lies ;
Thy table's loud clash and thy stink pots to smash,
Bloody sconces and black hung'd-up eyes.

When thou birls't the brown browl, idiotic eyes roll,
Shedding round Pandemonium's light ;
The wine bottles reel and away angels steal,
Bidding reason and manhood * good night.

    * Intemperate drinking, eating, language, clothing, in fact, excess in the use of any good gift, is adverse to health, reason, and manhood— Misuse and non-use are twin evils.

THE WIDOWER.

——:o:——

    Once asking a young widower why he did not re-marry, he replied, "My wife is not dead"—being a christian you ought to know.

Love's witchery round beauty plays,
His shafts wing in a glance,
His smiles by spirit blinding ways,
Conceal his slow advance —
And love by winsome ways may try
His magic—but I know
No minion of the moon am I,
I'll go no more to woo.

One now among the Seraphim,
Came like the faithful dove ;
One seen in many an early dream,
Compell'd my soul to love.
She came like morning to the sky,
As lovely and as true ;
No minion of the moon am I,
I'll go no more to woo.

Within my arms, her sun went down,
The day I still deplore ;
For *true* love only *one* can own,
One only ko-i-noor.
Let others bury love—and soon
A roving lightly go ;
I am no minion of the moon,
I'll go no more to woo.

THE SPIRIT OF CHARLES DICKENS.

——:o:——

I live in the sunland of beauty and bloom,
Not dead as ye deem in the Abbey's cold tomb ;
Mourn ye for yourselves and your children mourn,
My labours are finished, I never return ;
I sleep not in death, but I live where the free,
And the fetterless flourish, then mourn not for me.

Lament for your lot, sad and weary that stay,
Pain's heritors—lodgers in dwellings of clay ;
Spectre haunted—your nights find you sad and forlorn,
And the foot-prints of death terrify in the morn ;
What heart ne'er conceiv'd, or eye saw now I see
The veil rent asunder, then pity not me.

I have found my soul's love 'mong the children of light,
Released like a child from the dragons of night ;
No cenotaph statue sarcophagus—tomb—
Erect for a friend who has only gone h me,
No catafalque pomp, or cortege let there be—
When my shell ye entomb—for ye bury not me.

Know ye where life's sunny rivers arise,
Saw ye where love lights the stars of the skies ;

Where the wicked molest not—the tempests are o'er,
, And the winter of earth-life afflicts us no more,
It is here—it is here, and since time first began—
Earth was not design'd for the homestead of man.

I have met kith and kin—greeted friends ever dear,
Here youth is eternal—love's climate is here—
I commune with the sages and seers of yore,
With bards, monarchs, heroes, call'd hither before ;
Sing jubilate ! Is it Thackeray I see ?
" Why my friend thou art bringing all Eden with thee."

A SCRIPTURE HYMN.

——:o:——

The followng hymn is a specimen of the thousand hymns which may be extracts altogether from the Word of God.

Bitter is my earthly lot.— Job, iii. 20.
I drink the wormwood bowl.—Lam. iii. 14.
Why art thou thus cast down so low.—Ps. xlii. 5.
Why art thou sad my soul.—Ezek. xiii. 22.

Although my friends avert themselves } Ps. lxxxviii. 18.
And from me all depart.
Thou Father in my darkest hour } Ps. lv. 22.
Wilt still sustain my heart.

Thou wilt not leave my soul in hell.—Ps. xvi. 10.
Or see me suffer wrong.—Acts, vii. 24.
Thou ever-more wilt be my joy } Ps. cxxxvii 6
My constant theme of song.

The finger of derision's sneer } Ps. cxiv. 51.
May point and wish my fall.
But thou wilt shut me safe within } Joel, ii. 23.
Thy Zion's hallow'd wall.

Go mark ye well her bulwarks,
And number all her towers ; } Ps. xlviii. 12.
Walk round about our Zion,
And know this God is ours.

His hosts in arms are terrible, } 2 Kings, vi. 7
His chariots rushing fire

His horsemen with their virgin hands, } Rev. xiv. 2.
Attune the golden wire.

My strength is all my Father's strength—Ps. xviii. 1.
His voice my voice shall be,—Ps. ciii. 20.
My pleasure His, my songs his praise } Ps. lxxi. 6.
Shall sound continually.

Awake ye dwellers in the dust, ⎫
God's body dead arise ;   ⎬ Isa. xxvi. 19.
Sing ! for thy dew is falling,   ⎪
Thy manna from the skies.   ⎭

HELL.

——:o:——

I DREAMT and the reason I only can tell,
But I had a most terrible vision of hell,
I went down a stair in pitch darkness and saw,
Yes I saw (which I know is no natural law),
A region so vast that my pulses were stay'd,
But a " White stone " I had, and I was not afraid.
And this I divulge for the use of mankind,
That the region I saw was the hell of the mind,
I saw Furies and Dragons, and Vampyres and Ghouls,
Deadlights and warnings, and Gabbleratch fowls,
Afrits of Eblis and Bugbear and Wraith,
Bulbeggars Goblins stood right in my path,
There were Kit with his candlestick, Hellwain and Spook,
Familiars and Fairies, and Pixies that knock,
And Brownies and Bogles, and Kelpies and Ghosts,
Elves Fawns, Evileyes, and Lemures in hosts,
The Spoorn and the Barghest, White Rabbit, Nightmare,
The old man in the oak, and the Satyr were there.
Mumbo-Jumbo, and Fetish, and Manitto stood,
With Lok, Joss, and Juggernaut cover'd with blood,
There were Doubles, and Deathwatches, Devils in blue,
And of Banshees and Changelings and Gnomes not a few.
Charms, Amulets, Philtres, and Witches I found,
And Pythoness, Wizard, and Augur around,
Magicians, Soothsayers, and Sorcerers great,
Fortunatus still standing by blind Luck and Fate,
Secondseers, Rhabdomancers, Ghostraisers in black,

And a Spaewife alone with a cat on her back.
There were Charmers and Empyrics, dark Necromancers,
Spells, Omens, and Periapts, evil Enchanters,
And Mystery sat in his robe like the night,
On his tripod essaying to juggle the sight,
With his Phantom of horror and Spectral thing,
Over all the mirk region the ruler and king.
And I stood till Aurora appear'd in the East,
And slowly progress'd in her bright golden vest,
And the Icons of horror and forms strange and wierd
In the mind's Sun uprising, like shades disappear'd,
Where hell reign'd was heaven, I woke and was fain
For that Sun in its rising will ever remain.
Mine eyes Christ has opened, whereas I was blind,
And I see the sad state of the night of the mind,
And the armies of horrors that harrow mankind.

DOOM OF THE YEAR 1870.

——:o:——

The songs of the glorious sons of morn,
Awoke at the year's advance ;
As he enter'd the temple of Capricorn,
On the chariot of Death and Winter borne,
In the change of the astral dance.

Mighty Sol sate in state on his throne,
With a crown of flame on his brow ;
And his presence with terrible majesty shone,
And the lightening flash of his eye was thrown,
On his systems expanse below.

Mercury smiled near the throne with spite.
At Mars in his panoply red;
Till Venus came round with her crescent light,
And Jove with his satellites show'd his might,
To Saturn crown'd with lead.

Ye hours lead in the old year,
And the hest of Sol was obey'd,
And the year seem'd haggar'd and pale with fear,
In his visionless eye was a frozen tear,
And a snowwreath wrapp'd his head.

Over Sol's face gather'd a frown,
As the storm broods to destroy,
" Speak dotard he thunder'd, with truthfulness own,
What down in thy Terra thy mission has done,
For thou wert but in my employ.

Hast thou made her sons more wise,
Are the fetter'd by tyrants free,
Is truth substituted for error and lies,
Hast thou opened Monarchs and minister's eyes,
Do nations more clearly see."

A shudder convulsed the form,
And the lips turn'd blue of the year,
And he glared as we glare at an imminent storm,
And mutter'd " Why shinest thou still on that worm
Called Man—who deserves no care."

Ho ! Chaos and Night come forth,
(They came at Sol's dread command)
Give this wretch in your bottomless dungeon a birth
Drive him down with the lovers of darkness on earth,
With your hurricanes four in hand.

Round, Sol then the planets began,
Again the lavolt of mirth,
And threading strathspeys to Apollo, they ran,
And a year was elected more friendly to man,
And commission'd to govern earth.

THE WEAVER.

———:o:———

Treddle and drum, nipping and thrum,
Breast beam and back, edging too slack,
Coppings too tight, bobbins not right,
Rattletraps clash, ends all to smash,
Picking-sticks rap, shuvel and trap,
Bad weft and warp, size dry and sharp,
Clatter along : listen the song—
Nickity knack, nickity knack,
Jenny loves Johnny, and Jenry is bonny,
And Johnny will never deceive her ;
Nickity knack, nickity knack,
Tom, Dick, and Harry, whenever they marry,
Have promised to marry a weaver.

Back rods and reeds, temple and thread,
Raddle and coil, feather and oil,
Pulley and wheel, hank on the reel,
Slayboard and shed, shuttlebox thread,
Nippers and knot, scratching a spot,
Shuttles go glib, roll on the web,
Driving along: on with the song—
Nickity knack, nickity knack,
Jenny's got Johnny, and Jenny is bonny
And Johnny is not a deceiver ;
Nickity knack, nickity knack,
Tom, Dick, and Harry to-morrow will **marry,**
And heigho for love and a weaver !

THE NIGHTINGALE AND CUCKOO.

A FABLE.

A NIGHTINGALE and cuckoo long
Had disagreed about their song ;
The nightingale, in long oration,
Pleaded all his variation,—
His tones of love, and joy, and fear,
Now mournful trill'd, and now severe ;
Of high and low, and clear and free,
Attun'd in choral harmony ;
And argued, if 't was put to test,
His surely would be judg'd the best.
Think how the cuckoo star'd and rav'd,
To be by such a thing outbrav'd ;
A little, puny, grey hedge-bird
To talk so lofty, 'pon my word !
Anger prompted, at the challenge,
To tear the braggart with his talons ;
But chocking it, he scream'd "proud creature,
Direct we'll choose an arbitrator,
To judge my notes, by old and young
So lov'd, so listen'd to and sung :
That being agreed without division,
They flew to seek some learn'd decision,
And happen'd, ere one well had spoken,
To wing close by a hedge just broken,
Where an ass was feeding rarely,

Though thievishly, upon some barley ;—
" Hollo !" the cuckoo cries, " my friend !"—
Poor donkey almost stood on end,
Thinking t' was the farmer come
With mighty hedgestake and his doom ;
But seeing that his fears were vain,
He shakes his ears and eats again ;—
" Here's Philomel in high dispute,
And I,—we hope our humble suit
Will not offend,—about our song
We can't agree ;—we wont be long ;
And you shall hear us and decide ;
Your judgement cannot be denied ;
Your ears are longest, surely they
Were made for music every way."
" Well," snorts the ass, " go on, go on,—
I'll list a moment, till you've done ;
I've tasted nought—God help my fettle—
This day but one poor wizen'd nettle ;
And now your bother's come, when fairly
I'd burst my hide upon this barley."
The nightingale turn'd all his strains
Of river-song, and woods, and plains ;
The other, neither harsh nor low,
Twice or thrice sung out " cuckoo !"
" Well," says the ass, " for variation
Philomel holds the highest station ;
But should he think he beats he's wrong,
For I prefer a good plain song."

THE END.

Contents.

J

146

147

148

PAGE.

www.ingramcontent.com/pod-product-compliance
Lightning Source LLC
Chambersburg PA
CBHW020234030726
47497CB00009B/3096